Books By Keely Brooke Keith

Uncharted

The Land Uncharted
Uncharted Redemption
Uncharted Inheritance
Christmas with the Colburns
Uncharted Hope
Uncharted Journey
Uncharted Destiny
Uncharted Promises
Uncharted Freedom
Uncharted Courage
Uncharted Christmas
Uncharted Grace

Uncharted Beginnings

Aboard Providence
Above Rubies
All Things Beautiful

Want to be notified when Keely's next book is available?
Add your name to her email list at keelykeith.com/sign-up

Uncharted Courage

KEELY BROOKE KEITH

Edenbrooke
Press

Uncharted Courage

Cover designed by Najla Qamber Designs
Interior design by Edenbrooke Press
Author photo courtesy of Frank Auer

Printed in the United States of America

ISBN-13: 9798469655664

For Marty.

There are no words to express
the depth of my love for you.
Oh wait, apparently there are
Because I've written over a dozen novels out of that love,
and they just keep coming.

CHAPTER ONE

March 17, 2030
Almost autumn in the Land

The morning sun's first rays darted through the strong limbs of an ancient gray leaf tree that guarded the cemetery near Falls Creek. Bailey was supposed to be tacking her horse for the day's journey, but the gray leaf tree's intoxicating aroma made her linger in the graveyard as much as the man resting beneath the earth. Often, she had to remind herself that only her biological father's shell was buried below the stone marker, not his soul.

Last autumn, the earth had bulged unnaturally over Professor Timothy Van Buskirk's grave. The winter's heavy snows had since flattened the dirt, and spring's thick grass had grown over the soil. After a full summer of rain showers and sunshine and frequent mowing, the dried turf of Professor Tim's burial site now blended with the others in the cemetery, except for one fresh grave.

Bailey stood near Tim's headstone and allowed her gaze to drift up through the gray leaf tree's stalwart branches to a flock of geese passing high above. The honking birds, with their speckled feathers and long bills, didn't look quite like the geese back home in America, but they were fun to watch. The followers encouraged the leader as it cut a path through the air, guiding them northward for the Land's warmer temperatures. Though the official beginning of autumn was still days away, the Antarctic winds were already changing, hinting at a fast-approaching winter for the Land.

At least that was what every trader who passed through the village of Falls Creek said.

John Colburn's invitation for an extended visit in Good Springs couldn't have come at a better time for Bailey. Though their correspondence had been steady—thanks to Revel's reliable courier service—there was still only so much of John's wise counsel she could absorb from his letters. She needed to spend time with him in person, having fireside conversations in his living room; eating slow, satisfying meals at his table; listening to his Sunday sermons from the family pew in the historic chapel.

Professor Tim had taught her all about plant biology back at Eastern Shore University in Virginia, and now she needed to learn deeper truths from John Colburn—truths about God and life. Hopefully, she would also discover the source of the nagging yearning she couldn't name or define. She stooped to trace a reluctant finger over the carved letters of Tim's headstone. "I'm sure you would understand, Dad."

It still felt weird to call Professor Tim that. She hadn't even known he was her father until days before his death.

The stone's coolness chilled her finger. She withdrew her hands into the sleeves of her old E.S.U. sweatshirt. Autumn would be warmer in Good Springs than here.

Maybe it would feel like her college nights back home on Virginia's coast. Those nights seemed like a lifetime ago.

She shouldn't conjure memories of the past, of her life before coming to the Land. When she competed in martial arts tournaments in high school, Coach had always said champions never looked backed at failure, only forward for the win. He was right. She should only think of how grateful she was for her new life here—no matter how much it had cost.

She stood, her vision locked on Tim's headstone.

He had made all this possible for her by giving his life to get her across the world to this magnificent, hidden land.

Her new life came with her dream job, a peaceful community, new friends, and even distant relatives she hadn't known about until this time last year. "Thank you, Dad," she whispered to the empty air as she stepped back. "I'll be back in a few weeks."

Soft sunlight crept higher over the horizon, shining on the freshly harvested fields that stretched across the rolling hills. She loved this region of the Land. Time away might make her love it even more, which would be helpful if Falls Creek was in for the hard winter the traders were predicting. She would be back before then, ready to prep the greenhouse for a winter crop, ready for long nights of telling stories and playing cards with the people she'd grown to love at the inn.

Soft boot thumps rustled the dry grass behind her. That casually shuffling gait always warmed her heart. She turned to watch Revel Roberts cross the cemetery toward her.

He waited until he was close enough to speak in the private tone he reserved for her. He gave Tim's headstone a quick glance. "I don't want to rush you, but the McIntoshes are eager to leave soon."

The family of four was climbing onto their covered wagon near the stable block. Revel's brown stallion stood beside it, proudly facing the road. Bailey couldn't see her horse from here. "Okay, I'll be right there to saddle Gee."

"No need. I already have." The sun ascended a degree and shone on Revel's clean-shaven face. He didn't look away from her, but only squinted, crinkling the skin around his caring eyes. "Take your time here. I'll get your bags."

He always did too much for her. His gentlemanly manners were charming, but she could take care of herself. "No, Rev. You're sweet, but I'll get my stuff when I go inside to say goodbye to Eva and Sybil."

He lifted his chin at the laundry house across the yard. "I saw Naomi go in there a few minutes ago."

"I said goodbye to her after breakfast. To Claudia too." She took another step back from Tim's grave. "I just came here to tell… not that he can… it's just that—"

Revel ran an understanding hand over her shoulder. "I know." His gaze turned to the newest tombstone on the other side of the cemetery.

Maybe he had walked to the cemetery to do more than hurry her along. She motioned toward Frederick Roberts' grave. "You probably want a few minutes alone."

"No. My father isn't here. He's much happier where he is." He snapped his eyes away from Frederick's headstone. "He's back to his healthy self, energetic and in his right mind."

The look he gave her then said all she needed to hear and asked for all she could not give. Her insides tightened like they had the time he attempted to kiss her.

The time she turned him down.

Before she could back away or think of something diverting to say, the pleading in his gaze departed. He ran a knuckle along her sleeve. "I just wanted to make sure you're all right."

"Yeah, I'm fine. Super. Couldn't be better."

He lowered his chin and gave her the *Oh, really?* look she deserved.

They had more in common now that he too had lost his father. The comfort of having a kindred spirit softened their shared grief. That was something she'd never had with any of her guy friends back in America, even the teammates she'd fought alongside in tournaments.

The playful yelling of two small children carried across the yard. Revel's expression lightened as he pointed a thumb back at their fellow travelers. "The McIntoshes are hoping their little ones will fall asleep when the wagon starts rolling."

Bailey chuckled at the excited kids. "I don't know much about kids, but I think it will take more than a rolling wagon to persuade them to take a nap. Maybe I'll slip them a cup of gray leaf tea."

Revel's eyes widened briefly before he smiled.

She loved when her humor shocked him. Yes, she would have fun on this trip. With renewed excitement for the journey, she started for the inn's side door. "Tell the McIntoshes I'll be right there. Just a quick goodbye to Sybil and Eva, then we can hit the road for Good Springs." She hollered to him over her shoulder as she jogged to the inn. "Road trip to Good Springs! Woo hoo! This is going to rock!"

He left the graveyard without giving his father's tombstone another glance. "To rock? Is that good?"

"It is!"

"Excellent! To rock, it is." A hint of mischief curved his lips and filled his eyes with delight. It was a look he gave her often, and she hoped he always would.

* * *

Revel waited until Bailey was inside the house before he glanced back at his father's grave. She'd been through enough hardship in the past year—in her life, really—that he didn't want to give her more concern. She didn't need to know how difficult it was for him to leave this place now, seeing as how all his father ever wanted was for him to live at Falls Creek.

No one needed to know.

He couldn't permanently stay anywhere now that everyone in the Land relied on his courier service, nor did he want to. He was made for the road. Besides, he had worked it all out with his family and received his father's blessing months ago.

It still hurt to leave his childhood home. It wasn't something he could explain to himself, much less to a woman like Bailey.

A woman like Bailey. There was no such thing. There was Bailey Colburn and no other. God made her, then He burned the pattern.

Revel looked away from his father's tombstone, hoping no one had noticed him pause there. With a swifter pace, he returned to the stable block. The family he was escorting to Good Springs was already seated on their wagon's bench—the mister holding the reins, the missus clutching their little girl on her lap, the wiggling little boy lodged between the parents.

An uninvited vision flashed through Revel's mind. Instead of the McIntoshes sitting on the wagon bench, it was him and Bailey with their own little ones between them.

He silently rebuked the impossible wish as he untied Blaze's line and checked the saddle straps while he waited for Bailey. Soon, she hurried out of the inn and across the yard, carrying the black backpack she'd brought to the Land. She traveled lighter than any woman he knew, both physically and emotionally. No matter what she endured, she seemed to recover with a well-disciplined ease that almost made him envy her years of athletic training.

He hadn't known things like competitive fighting existed until he met her. He didn't know a lot of things existed until he met Bailey.

She flipped her cropped sable hair off her forehead as she secured her backpack to Gee's saddle. "Thanks for waiting, guys. So, who's ready for an awesome road trip?"

Mr. and Mrs. McIntosh exchanged a curious glance. It was always enjoyable to watch people's reactions to Bailey's odd expressions. And to her strong opinions.

She was right: this trip would be great. Though Revel's reasons for looking forward to it probably differed from hers.

"Get on up!" Mr. McIntosh yelled at his pair of draft horses, and they steadily pulled the wagon away from the stable block.

Revel swung into his saddle and clicked at Blaze. Hesitation pulsed through his horse's lean muscles. He too would rather lead than follow, but Mr. McIntosh requested Revel ride behind them in case they lost anything from their over-loaded wagon. The bartered exchange for escorting the relocating family to Good Springs was well worth the slow ride behind them. Revel was looking forward to receiving the new leather mailbag Mr. McIntosh promised him.

Bailey brought Gee up beside Revel, and they rode well behind the rickety wagon in case something did fall from it. When they rounded the front of the inn and crossed the stone bridge, Revel gave one last wave to Sybil and Eva, who stood on the front porch with aprons on, ready for a full day of work.

He missed his sisters every time he left Falls Creek, which only made his brief visits here that much sweeter.

Bailey waved too, then gave him a rascally grin. "So, which one of your sisters do you think will get pregnant first?"

He almost swallowed his tongue. "The things that come out of your mouth, woman."

She shrugged, still grinning. "What's the big deal? Eva has been married to Solo for four months, and Sybil and Isaac have been married three. I can't turn a corner inside the inn without bumping into some kissing couple. You know one of them must have a bun in the oven by now. Probably both."

He craned his neck to see around the covered wagon, but the McIntoshes weren't visible from back here. Hopefully, they couldn't hear Bailey's indecorous banter over the rattling of their wagon or the squealing of their lively children. "If or when either of my sisters becomes… finds she is… with child, it will be announced at the proper time."

"Come on, Rev. You know you've wondered too."

"You won't make any new friends on this trip if you talk like that in front of the McIntoshes, especially if their children hear you." He didn't need to look at Bailey to know her expression hadn't changed. "And that smirk doesn't make it easy for me to lecture you."

The wagon hit a dip in the road, and both of its back wheels screeched.

Bailey shooed a hand at him. "Don't sweat it. They can't hear me up there for all that noise."

He held his response for a moment, just as his father did when he corrected him as a child. It made him itch. He wasn't his father, and Bailey wasn't a child. Besides, he found her blatant curiosity as appealing as her figure. He kept his voice quiet. "Probably Sybil."

"Hm?"

"I think Sybil will be blessed first."

Bailey nodded. "Yeah, I think so too. She and Isaac can't keep their hands off each other."

He would never get used to Bailey's indelicate comments. The humor pulsed off her, but his eyes refused to look. If he did, he would certainly laugh, and that would only encourage her. He forced a straight face and stretched his riding gloves, even though they didn't need stretching. "Only time will tell."

"Yep."

"Let's leave it at that."

"Okay." Her grin didn't fade. "If you say so."

"I do."

"Fine."

"Fine."

A day of riding behind a crawling wagon would have tried his patience, but with Bailey next to him, time couldn't pass slowly enough. After a night spent in guest rooms in Woodland and a second day on the road, they reached the last campsite before Good Springs.

Revel stayed by the fire long after the others had gone to bed. A single log burned in the stone pit at the center of the circle of stumps travelers used when they stopped here. He'd camped at this site countless times; however, tonight he couldn't sleep.

A sharp snore came from the McIntoshes tent. The sound wasn't what kept Revel awake. He glanced at the center tent in the group's three canvas shelters. He had spent nearly a year analyzing Bailey's every word, hoping for a sign their relationship would grow beyond friendship. He often imagined their future together, but it seemed hopeless considering her frankness about her desire to stay single.

Now, both of his sisters were married and his younger brother, James, would be soon. Seeing others find their soulmates didn't used to make him yearn for the same happiness. But now that he loved Bailey, watching his siblings enjoy lifelong commitments only pricked his aching heart.

Even though Bailey was unattached, she never expressed a hint of loneliness. Her fierce independence made her different from every other woman he knew. It made him love her, but was also what kept her from needing him.

And how he yearned for her to need him!

Even on this journey, whenever he checked on her while they rode, she said she was fine. Every time he offered her assistance when they set up camp—whether it was with hammering a tent stake or untacking her horse—she said she could manage by herself.

And she could. Maybe that's what was so frustrating.

He looked away from her tent and sent the glowing end of his iron poker into a bucket of water that was waiting to extinguish the campfire. It hissed loudly. The snoring paused.

He hadn't meant to wake anyone—certainly not the children. He should put the fire out and go to bed. Just when he shifted his weight to rise from the stump he was using for a chair, Bailey's tent door opened. She closed the tent flap behind her and flipped her hood over her head. The firelight brightened her face angelically, but a scowl marked her expression as she walked toward the campfire.

Revel's mind cleared of every other thought. "What's wrong?"

"Nothing." She retracted her hands into the sleeves of the oversized sweater she'd brought to the Land. On the front of the sweater, block letters spelled out the name of the university she'd attended in America.

He stood and opened his hand to offer her his seat. As she sat on the good stump, he lowered himself to the splintery stump next to it. At least she'd learned to accept his small offerings of kindness.

He kept his voice down as not to wake anyone. "Did the snoring bother you?"

Just as he asked the question, a raucous rumble came from the McIntoshes' tent.

Bailey rolled her lovely eyes. "There's always one snorer, isn't there?"

"I think it's Mrs. McIntosh."

She quietly chuckled. "Those poor kids."

The fire's smoke spiced the air, and its soft glow highlighted Bailey's features, making her seem delicate and defiant all at once. He tried not to stare. "Why couldn't you sleep?"

She poked her ring finger out of her sweater cuff and started biting her nail. "The tent is so… confining."

"Still hate sleeping in a tent?"

She nodded. Her amber eyes peered at him from under her hood. "So, why couldn't you sleep?"

He almost claimed he could've slept just fine if he wanted to, but he was already hiding the depth of his love for her. He needn't hide the real reason he was still awake. He pointed his poker stick at the McIntoshes' tent. "Their little boy came out of their tent and started to wander around. They slept right through it. I wanted to make sure he didn't do it again."

She glanced at the tent, then crinkled her brow at him. "You would make a great dad. Do you think you'll ever settle down and have a family?"

He only wanted to be a parent if he could share the experience with her. Still, he had learned to keep such comments to himself. "Someday. I'd like to raise kids."

An insider grin curved her lips. "That sounds nice to say that, but you don't want to give up your freedom any more than I do. That's why we get along so well."

"Because we are both selfish?"

"Everyone is selfish somehow. We're just selfish in the same way."

"Are we?" When she didn't answer, he swirled his poker stick in the dirt. "Until I met you, I thought all women wanted was a wedding and babies." His collar suddenly felt too tight, so he pulled it away from his throat. "And a husband to boss around."

She shook her head. "I'd rather have someone who truly understands me."

Maybe he had been wrong about the women he knew. When he thought of his sisters and their relationships, it wasn't the wedding they looked forward to, but the intimate love that grew in marriage. That was probably what women really wanted: to feel deeply loved. He held up an energized finger and tried again. "All right, what if you could choose between being deeply loved or being truly understood? Which would you want?"

She withdrew her hands into her sleeves. "Being understood."

His love for her and his knowing her wove together inside his chest. He caught her gaze and held it. "What if you could have both?"

A vulnerability hollowed her expression, making him almost regret his question. But if he was going to build something beyond friendship with her, he had to find his way into her barricaded heart.

Just when he thought he'd broken through, she looked away. "Yeah, sure. That's me. Love and understanding and dopey-eyed vows in a wedding chapel. Good one, Rev."

CHAPTER TWO

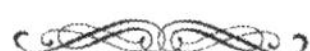

The instant the McIntoshes' wagon rattled out of the gray leaf forest at the outskirts of Good Springs, Bailey pulled on Gee's reins to turn off the road. "See ya later!" She waved to the family on their wagon bench as she trotted toward a paddock, ignoring her sore thigh muscles.

The children waved weakly, worn out by the long trip. Their parents repeated Bailey's goodbye phrase, then laughed at each other for using her dialect.

Bailey didn't say goodbye to Revel since she would see him at the Colburns' after he made his deliveries in the village. When she rose to give Gee room to gallop, Revel yelled, "Be careful, Bailey!"

She disregarded his warning and planned a speedy shortcut to the Colburn property. The tall grass crackled under Gee's powerful stride.

A deep inhale of the Good Springs air filled Bailey's lungs with the aromatic mixture of the gray leaf trees and the nearby ocean. Even though she had arrived in the Land only a year ago, that scent would always make her feel like this was home. The salty-minty combination flushed her mind of all doubt and worry, yet a pesky longing still murmured in her heart.

She slowed Gee as they approached a tree line between the empty fields. With the afternoon sun lowering to the west, her horse-and-rider shadow stretched along the recently harvested ground before them. Gee knew right where to go and trotted like a show pony in its debut performance. This horse was ready for a big bucket of the good oats her former owner kept in his barn.

"John will be happy to see you, girl." Bailey smoothed Gee's long mane. "And I'm excited to see him too."

It had been a long yet productive few months in Falls Creek. She'd learned how to live in harmony with the Land's culture—even if she still said things she thought were mundane but made the hearer's eyes bug out. She would always be an outsider, but she worked hard and they respected her for it. And the travelers she met at the Inn at Falls Creek found her to be an entertaining oddity.

The feeling was usually mutual.

During her time at the inn, her quiet life allowed her to recognize the mental effects of her childhood in foster care, her grief of losing Tim, and her guilt of surviving the world war, water poisoning, and plague while her friends and former classmates had not. She had made peace with all of that, yet still an unanswerable question lingered in her soul.

Time with John Colburn would help.

The open field led to a grassy paddock then to another field. After a quick cut down a forest-shrouded path, she was riding across the back of the Colburn property. Nothing much had changed since she was last here. The same stone marker carved with a C edged the boundary of John Colburn's ancestral homestead. The same woodpile rested near the same gabled barn, the same milk cow chewed her cud, the same chickens fluttered at her presence.

She jumped down from Gee and led her through the open barn doors. It took a moment for Bailey's eyes to adjust to the darkness inside. "Hello? Anybody in here?"

No one answered, nor was anyone visible outside Lydia's medical cottage or the big brick house. The kitchen door was open, so someone was home. The flowers that lined the flagstone path from the house to the cottage were fading from their summer glory and bowing their withered blossoms to deign to autumn's soon arrival. Maybe she would help Lydia prep her flower garden for winter.

Just because Bailey was taking a break from the inn didn't mean she expected to take a break from work. Especially when her work was also her passion. She patted her horse. "We're living the dream, aren't we, girl?"

Gee's hoof beats clopped casually as Bailey walked her into the center of the barn's open front area where she groomed her. After storing her saddle in the tack room, she led her horse to a stall for that promised bucket of oats.

Connor's stallion and Lydia's spotted gray mare were in their stalls, their horsey faces looking long and bored. The other stalls were empty, including John's. On Tuesdays he usually walked to his office at the chapel to study, so he must have ridden out to a congregant's home today. He was probably settling a village dispute or counseling a family from the church. As the village overseer, his duties seemed partially pastoral and partially mayoral. In the Land, that was all the governing they needed.

Wherever John was, he would return home at his leisure. No one here hurried much. Bailey had grown to love the soothing pace of life in the Land. She hooked her thumbs around her backpack straps and moseyed to the back door. The hearty aroma of a simmering stew wafted out of the warm kitchen into the cool near-evening air. She paused at the threshold. “Hello? It’s Bailey. Is anyone home?”

Lydia’s voice sung out from the living room. “Bailey!” Then her volume rose, but only as loudly as the demure village physician could courteously shout. “Connor, come downstairs, please. Bailey has arrived!”

The familiar American voice resounded from the home’s second story. “I’ll be right there!”

A muffled struggle and a kid’s giggle flowed from the living room. Exhaustion edged Lydia’s tone. “I’m coming, Bailey. Wait in the kitchen, please. Andrew and I are having a bit of a situation in here.”

While Bailey waited, she checked out the herbs Lydia was growing on the windowsill. Basil, sage, thyme, and several varieties of mint. She rubbed a peppermint leaf and smelled her fingertips. Sybil would be delighted to have more varieties for her cooking. Maybe Lydia would give Bailey some seeds to take to the greenhouse at the inn.

As she returned to the doorway, a toddler with jet black hair and no pants sprinted from the living room into the kitchen, squealing with slobbery kid laughter. Lydia hurried in behind him, holding tiny pants in one hand and pushing sweaty strands of light brown hair off her face with the other.

When the little boy met Bailey's gaze, he halted and stared up as if she were an intruder. His smile dissolved.

Lydia shook her head at him. An exhausted motherly grin warmed her eyes. "Now, Andrew, is that any way to welcome our distant cousin?" She paused the battle with her half-naked son for a moment and hugged Bailey. "It is good to see you. And please, do excuse his appearance. Since he doesn't need diapers anymore, he has decided pants are optional too."

Bailey didn't know when kids were supposed to be potty-trained or how mothers made that happen. And since she had accepted a government-funded sterilization to secure a college grant in the Unified States, she would never get to find out. But champions didn't waste energy on regret; they focused on what was before them. She gave Lydia's arm a gentle squeeze. "It's good to see you too."

Lydia leaned out of the kitchen and aimed her voice up the polished staircase. "Connor, do come down, please."

"I'm almost done, babe."

She gave Bailey an apologetic smile. "He's unclogging the bathroom sink. We left Andrew alone in the bathroom for two minutes and he crammed a whole jar of cotton balls into the drain."

The little boy giggled with the kind of naughty happiness that made Bailey both yearn to be a parent and relieved not to be one at the same time.

Lydia reached for Andrew, but he dodged her kind hand. He took off around the long kitchen table, passed by the stone hearth, and shot back into the living room, wearing only a tiny cotton shirt befitting a baby pilgrim.

Bailey laughed. "I see he takes after his daddy." When Lydia crinkling her logical brow, Bailey clarified. "Not because of the missing pants… I meant because he's curious and… evasive."

"Oh!" Lydia's smile returned. She tossed the little pair of trousers into the living room. "Yes to each quality in equal measure. Our Andrew is the most intelligent two-year-old I've ever known, and he's also the most daring. I'm not sure how we'll manage him when he—"

"When he what?" Connor asked, carrying a fully clothed Andrew into the kitchen. He held the boy firmly, despite Andrew's attempts to break free from his father's loving arms. "We'll manage just fine, Doc. Always have, always will." He winked at Lydia as he passed her, then gave Bailey a churchy, one-armed side hug. "What's up, Jeans?"

"Not much." She pulled away when Andrew poked her cheek with a sticky thumb. "Eva gave me a break from the greenhouse for a few weeks and your awesome father-in-law invited me here."

"We're glad Eva could spare you." He straightened the chairs around the table, which his son had shoved during the high-speed escape. "Lydia and Sophia have been eager to work with you on their latest gray leaf research project."

Andrew gave up his struggle. He nestled his head against his father's shoulder and popped his thumb into his mouth.

That explained the sticky thumb print still moist on her cheek. She wiped it with the back of her hand. "Yeah, me too. The research notes they sent me were really intriguing."

Lydia lifted the lid from a stock pot on the stove and gave the stew a stir. "Every time Revel comes through Good Springs, he gives us a full report on the number of gray leaf tree saplings you've grown and sent to the western villages. We're so proud of the work you're doing for the Land."

Connor opened a cupboard and grabbed dishes with one hand, Andrew content in the other. "I heard over a hundred trees were planted between Riverside and the mountains since the start of summer."

Bailey hadn't done the work for the praise but to protect the Land. Still, it was nice to have her efforts acknowledged. "It was up to one hundred forty after the last batch I sent."

"Good work." Connor pointed at her backpack on the floor by her feet. "Lydia has your old bedroom made up for you. Get settled in. John should be home soon, and then we'll eat."

"Thanks," she said, eyeing the pot Lydia was stirring. "It smells fantastic."

Lydia tapped the drips from her wooden ladle. "This was my Aunt Isabella's favorite stew." She replaced the pot lid. "Towels are in the linen cupboard in the guest washroom. You might want to avoid the upstairs bath while you're here since you-know-who," she pointed the ladle at Andrew, "is full of surprises."

"Got it. Thanks." Bailey watched them for a few seconds longer while Connor and Lydia carried on with their routine of making dinner and talking in half sentences only they understood.

As she walked through the living room toward the bedroom she'd stayed in when she first came to the Land, she glanced back at the young family once more, and something in her soul whispered, *If only...*

* * *

After dinner, Revel followed Connor outside to help with the evening chores while Bailey and Sophia cleaned the kitchen with John, and Lydia took little Andrew upstairs for a bath. The child had ended the meal with more stew on his clothes than in his stomach. It made Revel miss his visits to the inn back when his nephew, Zeke, was that age. Hopefully, he would have more nephews and nieces soon, like Bailey had suggested.

Daylight resigned to dusk during dinner, and the evening air cooled quickly, prompting John to close the usually open kitchen door behind Revel and Connor. It was just as well: Revel needed to speak to Connor privately.

He gave the road and the moonlit medical cottage a quick check for anyone who might overhear him. Since no one was around, he didn't wait until they reached the barn to ask Connor a most pressing question. "Will the security team be active tomorrow night?"

Connor's ever-vigilant gaze swooped from one side of the Colburn property to the other. "Yes, but not like last year."

Revel's wrong move when Bailey and her friends came to the Land had set off a firefight on the shore that left three outsiders dead, one missing, and Bailey wounded. His guilt had since simmered to a low burn, but if more outsiders invaded with guns drawn again this year, he would defend the Land just as passionately—albeit with more discernment and controlled marksmanship. "Tomorrow will be the autumn equinox. It's the only day of the year when outsiders have ever entered the Land."

"I haven't forgotten." Connor's controlled voice didn't waver. "Never will."

It had been five years since the former Unified States pilot parachuted to the shore here, healed from his wounds, and became a pillar of the Good Springs community. Two years ago his co-pilot, Justin Mercer, found his way back to the Land but then left, dissatisfied with the culture's traditional values. Revel didn't meet the man then, but had heard all about him since. And last year Bailey and her group entered the Land on the equinox.

Bailey he loved; it was some of the others in her party that made him nervous for the Land's safety this week. "More outsiders might be trying to come here."

Connor squared his shoulders. "Remember, our security team exists to help the Land *without* hurting others."

Revel hadn't forgotten the team's new focus, which was due to the Land's leaders insisting on pacifism. "I don't want the overseers to shut us down again either." He glanced back at the house as if he could see Bailey through the brick walls. He imagined her in the kitchen, contentedly chatting with John. "I just want to protect what is important, who is important."

"Likewise." Connor struck a match and lit an oil lantern on the workbench inside the barn. While the flame danced to life, Connor lowered his voice. "I've already spoken to the other men on the team. Everyone is to stay vigilant tomorrow during the day, and we are each taking a two-hour watch tomorrow night."

"At the shore?"

"No. From our houses."

"How can we protect the Land from intruders without being at the entry point on the shore?"

"Simply stay outside and listen for anything peculiar."

Revel remembered the eerie flashes that came from the guns last year on the shore and the feel of the bark along his skin as he hid behind a pine tree and aimed his crossbow at the two violent intruders in Bailey's group. He rubbed his sleeve to make the memory go away. It didn't work. It never did. "We should patrol the shore. Everyone who has come to the Land, entered on the shore in the same area."

A shadow deepened the crease over Connor's raised brow. "What about all those ship remnants on the beach below the cliff on the other side of the mountains? Those people entered the Land's protected atmosphere somewhere other than at Good Springs' shore."

"Or they entered here at Good Springs and drifted around the Land close to shore like Bailey's father did."

"Not likely."

"Even so, they didn't make it far into the Land. Not even over the mountains."

"Thanks to those poisonous vines."

Revel opened his mouth for a quick reply, but stopped. Connor was sly about steering a conversation, but there was real danger here last year. Revel steadied his tone. "The possibility of more violent intruders shouldn't be ignored simply to appease the overseers. You taught us always to be on guard during the autumn equinox at Good Springs' shore. Has something changed?"

"Just in my heart." He pointed up. "The Lord is teaching me I can protect the Land *and* help anyone who comes here for refuge."

"The crewmen who came to the shore with Bailey last year weren't here for refuge. They shot at every shadow. And they aren't the only outsiders with boats or aircraft. Have you heard any more radio transmissions or flyovers?"

The curved lines on Connor's face straightened. "No. Nothing in three months."

"We should have armed men patrol the shore tomorrow night."

Connor shook his head once, and his eyes narrowed a warning for Revel to back down. "We must be prepared, but not anxious. Two-hour shifts, someone listening all night from their home. Each man on the team is to have his horse saddled and his crossbow ready, but that's it. Have faith, Rev. It'll be okay."

Despite Connor's insistence, Revel wasn't convinced. But at least they were doing something to protect the Land. "Very well. When is my watch?"

Connor lifted the lantern and rattled off the team members' schedule as he walked to the horse stalls. "Levi is covering the six to eight P.M. shift. Everett chose eight to ten. Nicholas wanted ten to midnight. I'll take midnight to two A.M. watch. Can you handle the four A.M. to sunrise shift?"

"Of course. What about the two to four watch?"

Connor scooped oats into feeder buckets for the horses. "Mark Cotter was going to take it, but he hurt his back. I was thinking about asking Bailey to cover that shift."

"That's a good idea." Revel lifted a full bucket and carried it to Blaze's stall. "Bailey will enjoy that."

* * *

Bailey tucked her fingers into her sweatshirt's warm sleeves as she followed Connor and Lydia across the Colburn's moonlit property to cut through the forest for a bonfire on the beach. Revel stayed close behind her. His hovering didn't bother her as much as it used to. It was kind of comforting to have someone always looking out for her, like she imagined it would be to have a big brother.

Wood smoke wafted down the forest path on the ocean wind, exciting her as the dried pine needles and loose sand shifted under her hiking boots. Ahead, Connor stepped out of the forest first, then Lydia. Moonlight widened Bailey's view of a cozy beach fire surrounded by a semicircle of log benches. Everett and Bethany were seated on one, and Levi and Mandy were nuzzling on another. Connor and Lydia took the center log and left the fourth open.

Bailey loved life at the inn, but in Falls Creek she didn't have the luxury of hanging out at the beach like this. She looked back at Revel. "This is awesome!"

He matched her smile, delighting her heart. "Wait until you hear the stories Connor tells around the fire."

"I've heard him tell stories before."

Revel chuckled once. "Not these stories."

As soon as Bailey reached the circle, Bethany jumped up to give her an excited hug. "Oh, Bailey! I'm so happy you came for a visit!" The youngest Colburn daughter was by far the tallest, and the most demonstrative.

"Absolutely nothing thrilling has happened in Good Springs since you left."

Bailey wasn't sure if she should take that as a compliment, considering what happened last time she was in Good Springs. "Um, hopefully nothing thrilling will happen while I'm here this time."

Bethany giggled and released her from the girlish hug. "It's exciting just to have you here."

Levi rolled his eyes at his younger sister, then he reached out to Bailey for a fist bump while she passed his seat. "You're in Good Springs to beat up on Connor again, aren't you?"

Connor chortled. "She didn't get a single point on me last time we sparred."

Bailey couldn't resist. "And you didn't get a single point on me either."

Everett lifted his chin in greeting to her. "Sounds like a rematch is in order. And maybe Revel will stick around the village for a few days this time since you're here."

Revel faked punching Everett in the arm as he made his way to the only vacant bench. He touched the small of Bailey's back. "Let's sit as far from these troublemakers as possible."

Everyone was watching them as they settled onto the log. Revel sat close enough to her to make the other women exchange grins, so she slid a few inches away from him. She could handle the hope that lingered in his eyes—the hope that they would someday be more than friends—but she didn't want to spread the thought to anyone else.

Revel didn't flinch when she moved away. He seemed to have accepted that she wasn't looking for romance. And the fact that he understood her made her feel more loved than any boyfriend ever could. She waited for Connor to start telling his first story before she halved the distance between her and Revel. When she inched closer, he gave her a quick wink.

She'd come to tolerate those too.

Connor motioned with both hands as he built the tension in his clichéd campfire story. "And the frightened boy ran upstairs and locked his bedroom door. As he hid under the covers, he heard a scratching sound on the windowpane again and again." The whites of Connor's eyes gleamed as he clawed at the air. "Then suddenly lightning flashed outside and the window shattered. The boy peeled back the covers in time to see a figure slinking through the broken glass and into the bedroom. The furry creature stood like a man but had pointy horns and drooling jowls. Then the boy saw what was in the creature's hands. It was—"

Lydia sucked in a quick breath. Mandy hid her face with both hands, her red curls quivering like curtains shaking in a breeze. Bethany was smashed as close to Everett as possible and still squeezed her eyes shut.

Bailey almost groaned at the women's reactions at the dread of what the furry monster was carrying. She whispered to Revel, "I'll bet it's a pink umbrella."

"Shh," Revel nudged her gently while stifling a smile.

Connor didn't hear them or acknowledge it if he did. "It was the cherished hat the boy's father had been buried with when he died years before."

While he finished his story to the squirms and gasps of the sheltered women and the grateful nods of the men they clung to, Bailey watched moonlit waves rhythmically roll onto the wet sand. If these women had been here on this wide beach one year ago, they wouldn't find Connor's silly stories so scary.

And Bailey's arrival in the Land wasn't even the scariest event she'd lived through.

But here in this peaceful place, a campfire story about a grave-robbing monster was enough to make Connor a storytelling legend. A legend that would immediately dissolve if these people ever saw television.

Everyone went quiet around her, so she looked back at Connor. He had one dark eyebrow raised at her. "Not scary enough for you, Jeans?"

There was no way she would burst anyone's bubble after they had so kindly invited her to their private party. She had watched Connor's stories acted out on the small screen dozens of times, mostly on the classics channel. She raised her sweatshirt hood to shield her bare neck from the chilly wind. "Yeah, sure. It was a great story, Connor. I've never heard it without commercial breaks."

That got a brief laugh out of him, and the others smiled though they wouldn't have understood. Then he leaned forward, and his smile faded. "All right, Jeans. If you don't like the old stories from back home, here's one you won't hear in the Unified States…

"Once upon a time, there was an uncharted island in the middle of the South Atlantic Ocean. It was hidden from the rest of the world by an atmospheric anomaly no one understood, but the inhabitants believed their secret world was providentially protected. They carried out their timeless agrarian lifestyle, oblivious to the world war raging around them… until one day when a navy pilot was ejected over their land. He descended to their shore and into the capable hands of the beautiful village physician." Connor pulled Lydia close, and the others made lovey-dovey *oohs* and kissy noises.

Bailey let her eyes roll. "Fascinating story, but it isn't scary. In fact, it's the opposite of scary. It's comforting."

He withdrew his arm from behind Lydia and propped his elbows on his knees, his eyes darkening as he peered at Bailey over the fire's orange flames. "You haven't heard the rest of the story."

Grins melted and uneasy glances flashed between the couples.

Bailey didn't mean to spoil their good time, so she lightened her voice with mock sweetness. "And everyone found their perfect match and married and had lots of babies and abundant crops and lived happily ever after. The end."

Connor slowly shook his head, his intense gaze only amplified by the flicker of the fire. "While the people of that hidden land were raising their happy families and plowing their fertile fields, there was a man on the other side of the world who knew their uncharted land existed. He had found his way there once and—"

Bailey wasn't about to let him use Justin Mercer to scare the others. "And that man swore he never would tell a soul about it."

Levi's low tone commanded attention. "But he broke that promise, didn't he?"

Lydia patted the charged air with both hands. "And the person he told is now safely in the Land with us, and we are grateful she is. No one else will ever know the Land exists, so let's have a new story, please."

There was no hiding that Bailey was an outsider. No matter what she had done for the Land in the past year, her arrival here would always be a strike on her record.

Agreement with Lydia cooled the heat in Connor's gaze. He returned his protective arm around Lydia's back, and a lazy grin softened his expression. "What I was going to say was… One day when that man was gazing at the stars and thinking of the perfect land he'd left behind, he noticed an odd star. It pulsed and its light turned a hazy blue, then it grew and grew until he had to look away. When he looked back, he saw a spaceship scorching the earth as it landed in a vacant lot nearby. He hid behind a splintery fence and watched as the spaceship opened and little green men walked out, holding laser guns."

Great. Now he was barfing up old science fiction storylines. The girls continued clinging to their guys, and Connor lost Bailey's attention. She watched the fire lick at the logs and thought about how Justin Mercer had promised John and the elders he wouldn't tell anyone about the Land. Levi was right: Justin had reneged on that promise when he told Bailey. And Justin also told her he wouldn't tell anyone else.

But what happened to the outside world after she came here? Had Justin Mercer kept his promise this time?

She faced the ocean where the water's gentle surface waves seemed as trustworthy as Justin's promises. Under those soft ripples churned a vicious current that had carried Tim's boat far down shore and took her biological father away.

She turned her face away from the ocean and glanced at Revel. He'd been there with her through it all. He was the first person in the Land to care about her, to see her as more than an invader. Now he was her best friend.

Before she could move her gaze past him, he looked down at her. With a half grin and a hand to her back, he reassured her of all that she couldn’t ask. Whether they were in Good Springs or back at the Inn at Falls Creek, to him, she belonged here.

And when he was close to her, she felt like she belonged too.

CHAPTER THREE

No one questioned Bailey the next morning when she slept late, nor when she sat in the living room reading long after the others went to bed that night. She would function better by staying awake until her two A.M. shift than by falling asleep for a few hours and then trying to rouse herself for duty.

And it worked. The house was still while everyone else slept. She laced her hiking boots and slipped into her sweatshirt while in the quaint old bedroom, then tiptoed down the hallway, through the living room, and into the kitchen. John had left an oil lantern burning low and a covered pan of some kind of oat casserole on the counter. She wasn't sure if it was edible now or needed to be cooked first. The dish's sugary-cinnamon scent was tempting enough to make her want to sample it. She reached for the pan, then paused.

Coach always said she fought better on an empty stomach because hunger made her mean.

She pulled back her hand, obeying his voice even if it was only a memory.

Those early morning martial arts training sessions back in her high school years felt like yesterday. But they weren't. That was years ago.

She wasn't awake at this hour to train for a match, yet covering a night watch for the security team gave her the same surge of anticipation. Not that she expected anything to—

The back door flew open with a clatter, pumping hot adrenaline through her system.

Connor smirked as he closed the door behind him and stepped into the kitchen. "Startled you, didn't I?"

"No."

"You flinched."

"Did not."

He lifted his chin at the casserole dish on the counter. "Want something to eat before your shift?"

"No, thanks."

"John made it."

"Not hungry."

"Suit yourself." He hung his jacket on a silver hook by the door and kept his back to her while he rummaged through its pockets. "Come back inside and eat if you change your mind. Just leave the door open so you can listen. It should be easy to hear if anything unusual happens. It's stone quiet out there."

"It won't be quiet at the beach. The waves don't stop crashing no matter what day of the year it is."

He snapped his gaze to her. "Don't go to the beach. You're only supposed to stay outside the house. That's what I told all the guys, and so far everyone has complied. We're only listening tonight. Staying alert but not anxious. Got it?"

It didn't matter if he was demanding total freedom or total submission, Connor was always demanding something of his team. Half of her pitied the guys who followed him like eager puppy dogs. The other half of her felt honored to be included in his pack, if only for one shift.

"All right, all right, I won't go to the beach."

"Or to the village."

"Fine."

"Stay on the property."

She mocked a military salute. "Yes, sir. I'll stay on the property, sir."

He tilted his angular chin. "This is serious, Jeans."

Apparently not if they weren't allowed to patrol the shore where anything would happen if it was going to happen. Then again, it was two in the morning and she didn't feel like arguing. "Don't worry. I've got this."

"Good." He toed off his boots and parked them in a row with several other pairs by the door. "I'll be upstairs if you need me."

"Don't worry, I won't." She raised her sweatshirt hood over her head. "And if you need me, I'll be on the beach."

"Real funny, Jeans." His voice sounded too tired for sarcasm as he traipsed out of the kitchen. Before he reached the stairs, he whispered over his shoulder. "Revel will relieve you at zero four hundred. Be safe."

When he ascended the stairs, his footsteps crinkled the floorboards as if he had sand on his socks. She tried not to imagine Lydia scolding him in the morning for tracking it through the house.

Bailey left the kitchen lantern burning low as John had instructed them all to do during this uncertain night. As she pulled the door closed behind her, a sprinkling of sand that had fallen from Connor's boots crunched under her shoes.

It was eerily quiet outside, just as Connor had said. The oval moon's full light gave the yard a mystic glow. Crisp night air chilled her face as she scanned the property. The dry grass flattened under her feet. Its summer growth had encroached on the dirt driveway, but grooved wagon wheel tracks were still visible between the house and medical cottage.

She looked across the yard to the barn and the chicken coop, then walked to the corner of the house and surveyed all the way to the vegetable patch. Even though it was a short walk through a pine and gray leaf forest from the Colburn house to the shore, there wasn't much sand on the property—certainly not deep enough to get inside one's boots and stick to their socks.

Connor must have gone to the shore to have tracked so much sand into the house.

Well, since he hadn't stayed on the property during his shift, neither would she.

His other directives were acceptable. It was second nature for her to be alert without being anxious—that was the name of the game for champion fighters. That she could obey, but not staying on the property for two boring hours. If anything was going to happen on the equinox in the Land, it would happen on the other side of those trees.

Though the full moon gave enough light to see across the open lawn, the forest path would be dark. She felt the back pocket of her old blue jeans for her crank-powered flashlight and set out for the beach.

The log benches that the Colburn siblings and their spouses used for campfire nights were lined up along the tree line by the cairn. She stood in front of the ancient stack of stones which the founders had erected to mark where they had come ashore over one hundred sixty years ago. They believed God had protected them on their arduous voyage from America and brought them here to an uninhabited island for His purposes.

The generations that followed had intentionally built a God-fearing society that thrived in this isolated place. And until Connor arrived five years ago, the people of the Land didn't know how isolated they were or all that had happened in the rest of the world. John Colburn always said the Lord brought Connor here for a reason, and now her too.

She didn't deserve it. Just like she didn't deserve to survive the water poisoning and the plague and the world war. Nor did she deserve to be the only survivor in the group she came to the Land with. Her eyes drifted to the exact spot where the ocean's wicked current met the shore—the place where she'd met the Land—and the flying arrows from Connor's security team.

Even though it seemed odd for Connor not to be freaking out about invaders anymore, it was good that God had changed Connor's heart since her arrival. Better late than never. If Connor hadn't considered her group as a threat back then, maybe Tim and his nephew would still be alive.

If anyone came to the Land now and wasn't hostile, she would try to help them too.

She gave the softly glowing beach one last study. A few insomniac seabirds soared overhead, but otherwise the Land was sleeping. Connor was right: she shouldn't be out here. Everyone who took a shift tonight had simply stayed outside their home and listened. And nothing had happened.

Connor's men could trust his leadership, and so should she. More importantly, they all trusted God, and she was learning to as well.

The ocean breeze chilled her skin. She retracted her hands into her sweatshirt sleeves and hiked through the sand back toward the forest path. Moonlight caressed the cairn and made her pause, wondering how blissful life must have been in the Land before they knew about the condition of the outside world—before Connor arrived, then Justin Mercer, and then her group.

Ignorant bliss wasn't always a good thing. It was best the people here knew what was happening outside their happy bubble, and it was best they found out from a man like Connor Bradshaw, who cared about them and didn't want them exposed to a hostile world.

Her boots sunk into the thick sand as she hiked away from the shore toward the forest path. Just when she stepped on the first patch of fallen pine needles, a whirling sound vibrated the air behind her. She gave the ocean a quick scan and the beach as far as she could see in both directions. Everything appeared as it should.

The noise hadn't sounded like a bird or a sail flapping. More like electric fan blades whooshing in the distance. There were no electric fans or appliances or motorized machines here.

She was supposed to report anything unusual to Connor, but she couldn't report what she couldn't describe. The sound was so brief, she couldn't even tell where it came from. Besides, it was probably nothing.

Then again, she still had most of her two hour shift to kill. She might as well wander down the shore and take a look.

She withdrew her hands from her long sleeves and walked south along the tree line, avoiding the deep sand and the crackly pine needles. If the noise she'd heard had been made by a person, she didn't want them to hear her coming.

Before she reached the rocky outcrop where she would have to decide whether to walk on the wet sand by the ocean or hike inland to the top of the bluffs, she paused by the last pine tree. The seemingly gentle waves slipped onto the shore, pushing a crest of sea foam farther inland with each undulation.

The tide had turned.

If she continued walking along the beach, the incoming tide would trap her in the rocky caves below the bluffs, subjecting her to the violent currents that swirled around the Land.

An inland hike it was.

She tried to step lightly through the tall grass as the earth inclined, but with each step she cracked a twig or rustled the dried blades. If anyone had been with her, she would have laughed at herself for her poor stalking skills. Connor would have sarcastically called her a ninja. Revel would have asked what a ninja was. She would have to explain she was a competition fighter who'd trained in a city gym, not in a dark jungle or mountaintop temple or wherever ninjas learned to silently creep along like a hunting tiger.

Her heart picked up its pace with the hike, warming her blood. Hopefully, she'd get to take a few more of these hikes while she was in Good Springs, albeit hiking during the daytime would be more pleasurable.

She pushed up her sleeves as she neared the top of the bluffs. The view of the moonlit ocean from the cliffs would be worth the climb.

As she sank her heels into tussock grass for traction for the steep final steps, a muffled clatter of cracking sounds came from somewhere below the cliff. Then a hard thud and multiple splashes. Then silence.

If she had been anywhere else on the earth, she would have thought she'd heard a distant car wreck, minus the screeching brakes and honking horns.

With a surge of adrenaline, she sprang to the top of the cliff and inched close to its edge, peering down at the shore. Wave after wave rolled toward the rocks below. Whatever had made those sounds either landed in the ocean or was just out of sight on the sand between the water and the bluffs. She scanned the water from the sand all the way out to the inky horizon.

Maybe a huge nest of birds lived beneath the cliff and their nest had broken and crashed on the rocks below. She saw it once on a nature documentary. It could have been a nest of pelicans or seabirds.

She lowered herself to the rocky ground and leaned over the cliff for a better look. Each wave that splashed onto the rocks sprayed mist and foam into the air, scrambling her view. Moonlight glinted off the droplets of hazy mist that clouded between her and the shore below.

Something moved down on the sand. A bird? A shadow? She couldn't tell from up here. She needed to go back down to the tree line and jump from boulder to boulder to avoid the water so she could get a better look at whatever was happening below the bluffs.

Her feet followed the same path down that she had taken up, though at a much quicker pace this time. As she descended the grassy slope, she gripped her crank-powered flashlight but didn't turn it on. When she reached the bottom, a fallen branch caught under her boot. She steadied herself and slid the flashlight back into her pocket. If she lost it, she couldn't simply order a new one.

In the brief stillness of her pause, something rustled the brush ahead. A deer? A person? Maybe Revel had followed her, thinking he was being protective. If he had, she would be ticked. She didn't need his protection.

She tiptoed along the tree line as stealthily as possible, her heart rate increasing as she focused on the shadow. The closer she got to it, the more it retracted into the brush. It wasn't Revel; he was no coward.

She turned sideways to keep her body fully behind a tree trunk and peeked around it, waiting for the shadow to move. Her gaze traced the roundness of the bulk of the shadow and then followed it along the ground. Moonbeams highlighted the shapes at the end of two bent lines.

Feet. Booted feet. A man's booted feet.

She needed to get closer to be sure.

At first, she slinked along the tree line, but then it hit her: If this person was cowering, they were no threat to her. Probably just a young man from the village who had planned to meet his girlfriend down here and been startled when he saw someone patrolling the shore.

She stepped away from the trees and marched toward the crouching person. He had his arms covering his head, and the ends of the bush shook from his trembling.

As she stood over him, one branch hung between her and the person she was about to scold for his immature behavior. With a precise front-snap kick, she cracked the branch above his head, opening his hiding place.

The man flinched. He looked up at her with wild eyes. "Hide me!"

Dark hair covered his forehead and blood dripped from his broken nose. A full beard blackened the bottom half of his face, but she knew those eyes. Her racing heart lost a beat. "Justin?"

* * *

Revel threw off the quilt and rolled over to face the window in the guest room. He'd spent the last hour staring at the ceiling, praying no one encountered danger during their patrol tonight—especially Bailey.

Between the open curtains, the full oval moon inched across the sky. Two hours of sleep wasn't enough for him to function well for the rest of the day, but after hearing Bailey go outside, he would not sleep again until his watch.

The clock on the nightstand read half past two. His feet twitched, begging him to go make sure Bailey was all right. It would anger her if he did. She would say he was being overprotective, or worse, that he didn't trust her.

He would have to take the scolding because he simply couldn't stay in bed another minute. He raised his suspender straps over his shoulders and shrugged on a coat as he left the room.

An oil lantern burned on the table, softly lending its warm light to the quiet kitchen. He glanced out the kitchen door's window while he buttoned his coat. Bailey wasn't visible from the doorway. If he knew her—and he did—she was probably walking the property's perimeter, staying as far from the house as possible while still technically following Connor's orders.

He stepped outside expecting Bailey to pop out from behind the medical cottage and berate him for checking on her. Well, he wasn't. Not really. He just couldn't sleep and came outside for some fresh air.

Even he didn't believe that.

Thanks to the ample moonlight, the barn and road and paddock were clearly visible from here.

But no Bailey.

Revel walked around John's big brick house to check the back yard and vegetable garden.

She wasn't out there either.

As he turned for the front of the house, rustling came from the forest on the eastern side of the property. Surely Bailey hadn't gone to the shore. If she had deliberately disobeyed Connor's orders, he would never give her patrol duty again. He expected complete respect, and deserved it.

Maybe if Revel found Bailey and brought her back, they could keep her indiscretion between them. They'd done it before. She could trust him; he'd proven so.

He marched toward the trees and followed the sound away from the property. The stirring wasn't coming from the path that led to the shore, but from the south end of the property past the barn. There was a narrow path back there that led to the bluffs. Connor often took his telescope out there on clear nights. But Revel had heard Connor go up to his room after his shift, so it wasn't Connor. Maybe Bailey was walking that path.

Revel scanned the property in all directions and waited near the trees, listening. He heard nothing. It could have been a deer that rustled the forest.

No. Something wasn't right out here.

Though the temperature wasn't uncomfortably cold, a chill made him flip up his collar to cover the back of his neck.

He stayed on the edge of John's property and looked down the forest path but couldn't see far. A rooster crowed across the yard behind him, breaking the silence with its shrill cry. Revel flinched and held back a surprised curse. Some of the chickens started flapping around in their coop.

It was too early for that too.

Something had awakened them. Probably Bailey. She might be watching him from the shadows, laughing to herself.

He marched back to the house where he would wait for her. If she became angry with him for coming outside during her shift, he would tell her that he had to stand watch outside because she wasn't doing her job.

No, he didn't believe that either.

He would let her fuss at him for checking on her and laugh at him for being startled by a rooster. Then he would watch the moonlight hit her amber eyes while she smiled, and he wouldn't care what she was saying because the sound of her lovely voice was like a song he could listen to for the rest of his life.

That he believed more than anything.

Dried grass crunched under his feet as he marched across the lawn and stood near the kitchen door. The night no longer felt still. The chickens flapped in their coop, the milk cow paced by the paddock fence, and the wind swished through the gray leaf trees.

And then the gentle stirring of the trees turned into crackling twigs. It was more than the wind.

He watched the shadowy entrance of the path that lead through the forest to the shore. Whatever had been at the back of the property could have moved down to this path by now. He should get the oil lantern from the kitchen table and investigate.

As he reached for the kitchen doorknob, two dark figures emerged from the forest path. The first was Bailey; the second was a man walking closely behind her. Too close.

The darkness kept Revel from seeing the man's face across the distance. It didn't matter who it was. Bailey shouldn't be alone outside with a man at this hour.

Revel's fingertips curled into his fisted palms as he charged across the yard. "Bailey! What is going on?"

The whites of the man's wild eyes glinted in the moonlight as he reached for Bailey's arm. He wore factory-tailored clothing like Bailey wore when she arrived from the outside world, and he spoke with the same accent as Connor.

When Bailey yanked her arm out of the man's grip, Revel charged him. "Get away from her!"

Bailey stopped Revel with a hand to his chest. "It's okay. He's a friend." She glanced back at the bearded man. "Well, not exactly a friend, but I know him."

Blood dripped from the man's nose as he whispered with urgency, "Be quiet so he doesn't hear us."

Revel kept his eyes on the stranger but turned his chin to Bailey. "So who doesn't hear us?"

She ignored Revel's question and pulled the man's elbow, leading him toward the house. "Get inside so we can talk."

While they hurried to the house, Revel stayed within reach of the stranger and recalled every fighting technique Connor had taught him.

Bailey didn't look threatened, just annoyed. That didn't tell him much; Bailey never looked threatened and often looked annoyed.

She pushed open the door and kept her grip on the stranger's sleeve until they stepped inside. "Take off your filthy boots or Lydia will get miffed."

The man complied. "I know, I know."

Revel couldn't hold back his questions any longer. "Bailey, who is he?"

She looked at Revel—directly at him for the first time. "Go get Connor."

The man was crouched down, untying the thickest-soled boots Revel had ever seen. When he stood, he braced himself with his hands on his knees for a moment and breathed through his mouth.

The annoyance in Bailey's eyes softened. "Maybe you should get Lydia too. Just tell them to get dressed and come downstairs. I don't want to freak them out before they have a chance to wake up."

Though he loved her voice, sometimes he wished she spoke more plainly. "*Freak them out*?"

"Just go get them, please. I'll stay here with…" She looked down at the strange man then back at Revel, "with this traveler who needs our help and has been injured."

"Bailey, please tell me what is going on."

"I can't tell you because he hasn't told me yet. Just get Connor and Lydia, please." She gave him a look that begged for his trust.

It wasn't Bailey he didn't trust. While the man dabbed his bleeding nose, Revel looked at the woman he loved. "Very well. I will be right back."

CHAPTER FOUR

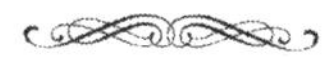

Bailey's heart thumped with determined pulses, flushing fiery blood through every eager artery. The instant Revel left the kitchen, she locked her gaze on Justin Mercer. "There. We're inside and the door is locked. Now tell me who you're hiding from and what you're doing here."

He peeled his hands off his knees and stood up straight, his balance wavering. Once he steadied himself, he lifted his bearded chin at her. "I came here to save you, beautiful."

"You're insane."

A tinge of humor permeated his weak voice. "I've been told that so many times in the last five years, I don't take offense anymore."

"You promised in the note you left in Connor's sunglasses case that you would make sure the Land stayed hidden."

"And that's what I'm doing."

"No, by coming here you're jeopardizing twelve hundred innocent lives. Most of the Land's inhabitants don't even know a world war is happening."

"By coming here I'm keeping you and all of them safe."

"We are already safe in the Land."

"Not for long."

Her hammering heart jolted. She drew a slow breath and straightened her spine to regain control of her nerves the way Coach taught her. It didn't work as well as it used to. "Will the Land be invaded?"

"Not by people."

"What's that supposed to mean?"

He shuffled the three steps to the back door as if every movement exhausted him. His volume decreased as he closed the curtains and peeked outside through a crack between them. "You don't know what has happened out there in the past year. When the belligerents started launching nuclear weapons at each other last week, the detonations triggered hundreds of volcanic eruptions, mostly around the Pacific Rim."

She tried to ignore the part about nuclear warfare, but her fingernails begged to be bitten. Somehow, she refrained. "We aren't near the Pacific Rim. The Land is in the middle of the South Atlantic Ocean."

"That doesn't matter to the earth's upper atmosphere. It's carrying an ever-thickening layer of volcanic ash across the globe right now. It will cover the sky above the Land within days. Scientists are predicting at least two years of hardly any sunlight getting through the particles anywhere on earth. The world is in for a big freeze. I came to tell Connor the Land should prepare for cold and famine."

When he turned away from the window, lantern light hit his face and illumined a purple line across the bridge of his broken nose. The panic in his eyes at the shore only moments ago had settled into a disoriented glaze. He whispered, "Man, I'm still seeing two of you."

She pulled a chair away from the table and pointed at it. "Sit down. You look like you might pass out."

He staggered to the chair, his strength a fraction of what it had been when she met him in Virginia last year. He'd said the volcanic eruptions started last week, but coming here would have taken him more than a week to plan and execute. He wasn't here to help; he was here for the only thing in the Land that he couldn't get elsewhere. She stared at him until she caught his eye. "You aren't here because of the eruptions. You're here for gray leaf medicine. What do you have? Cancer? Parkinson's? Heart disease?"

He leaned his head against the high back of the slatted wooden chair and closed his eyes. "Where's the doc?"

"Revel went to get her."

"Revel?" A sneer bolstered his faltering voice. "Is that your boyfriend?"

"Don't be a jerk."

"Oooo, Bailey's got a boyfriend."

She would have smacked him if he wasn't already in pain. "No, I don't have a boyfriend."

He peeped one eye open. "Don't worry, beautiful. When the big freeze comes, I'll keep you warm."

It was easier to verbally spar with Justin than to battle the nightmarish what-ifs swirling in her thoughts. She kept her voice flat. "You look like a half-dead mountain man, you're hiding from someone or something, and you still think you're God's gift to women?"

He raised a pathetic hand. "Relax, beautiful—"

Rapid footsteps thundered down the stairs, then Revel barged into the kitchen with a stern finger pointed at Justin. "I know who you are. You're the man who piloted the aircraft with Connor. You came to the Land once but left because you found us too moralistic for your taste. And then you met Bailey in America and—"

Bailey skirted the table and stopped Revel before he could pummel Justin. "Whoa, Rev. Chill out. He's injured."

More quick footsteps descended the stairs. Connor charged into the room, flashing past Revel and Bailey. "What the—" He controlled his tongue, but angry shock held his jaw half open. He halted inches from Justin. "You shouldn't have come back here, Mercer. You promised."

Justin dabbed his bleeding nose with the back of his hand. "If I had known the landing would be so painful, I probably wouldn't have come, especially with the greeting I've received so far."

Connor crossed his arms and stared down at Justin. "What landing? How did you get here?"

Justin tapped a limp finger on his chair. "Here?" He flicked a wrist at Bailey. "Your pretty little security guard rescued me."

At that, Bailey would have shoved Connor out of the way to get to Justin and choke the arrogance out of him, but his head dropped as he lost consciousness.

Connor caught his former co-pilot and kept him from slumping out of the chair. "Lydia!"

"I'm right here." The doctor wrapped her hair in a bun as she rushed into the kitchen. She checked Justin's pulse, rousing him enough to groan. A slight smirk curved his lips, as if this were a big joke. Maybe it was to him in his half-conscious state, but his arrival put the Land in danger.

Bailey wanted to blurt out all that Justin had told her about the nuclear war and the coming volcanic winter.

She held back. It would be better if Connor heard it from Justin himself. She glanced at Revel, and he met her gaze with concern in his eyes.

Her dear Revel didn't know what the Land was in for.

While Connor increased the lantern's light and held it close to Justin's face, Lydia lifted each eyelid, one at a time. After she examined Justin, she looked up at Connor. "He has a broken nose, multiple facial lacerations, and a concussion. He needs gray leaf medicine. We must take him to my office for stitches."

Justin's swimming eyes shot open. "No! I can't go outside. He will see me."

Lydia ignored his mumbled words and looked at Connor. "He needs gray leaf tea immediately." She struck a match to ignite the gray leaf chips in the stove's firebox, then filled a kettle to boil water.

While Lydia made the medicinal tea, Connor crouched to be eye-to-eye with Justin. "Who will see you if you go outside? Did someone come with you to the Land?"

"One of the Global men jumped into the two-seater with me just before I took off. It's a rickety, old helicopter our crew stole off a South African vessel last month." He lifted his chin, but closed his eyes. "That dinky chopper barely flew, but I knew it would get me here if we sailed close enough to the Land's entry coordinates. Don't worry, I removed the flight data recorder and disabled all the signal senders before—"

Connor yanked Justin's jacket open, revealing a black t-shirt with a Global insignia printed on it. His voice dropped an octave. "Are you working for Global?"

"We all are. The Unified States joined them months ago. When I learned Global was repositioning its South

Atlantic fleet to American ports in anticipation of nuclear war, I took a job as a communications technician on a repurposed Argentinian ship so I could come here and warn you. I ghost programmed the internal navigation systems to have us in the right place at the right time. Nobody on that ship had a clue what was going on. They thought the navigational controls were fried."

He chuckled to himself as if drunk. "Probably because that's what I made it look like. Volt taught me how to do that. Anyway, I planned to fly from the ship to the Land. Everything was going according to plan until a deckhand saw me start the chopper. He jumped inside. I thought he was going to try to stop me, so I took off. He shut the door just in time to keep from falling out over the water."

Connor cocked his chin. "What did the deckhand do?"

Justin's smirk grew. "He buckled his harness. What else could he do? We were here two minutes later."

Revel had heard enough. He rounded the table and stood behind Justin's chair. His chest rose and fell with a heavy breath as he glared at Connor. "What is he talking about? Will we be invaded?"

Connor slowly stood. He looked at Lydia, then Bailey, then put his hand on Justin's shoulder. "Will we?"

Justin shook his head so weakly if Bailey didn't know him, she wouldn't have been able to tell. "No one knows about the Land, except the deckhand who was in the chopper when I landed on the shore. Koslov is his name. Sergei Koslov. He was a hockey player or something like that before he was drafted for Global. Couldn't be sure. Super thick Russian accent."

Connor's nostrils flared. "When did Russia join Global?"

Justin looked up at Connor with fully opened eyes, the whites fearfully bright in the lantern light. "Russia didn't join Global. They started it."

Connor swallowed hard. His Adam's apple rose and fell before he spoke through clenched teeth. "Which countries haven't joined Global?"

"Everyone has joined, except China and their neighbors that they forced into an alliance."

After living through the water poisoning, plague, and war, Bailey was surprised at nothing that happened in the outside world—until this. World War Three had turned into a race for domination with Russia and their allies against China and theirs. The Unified States was nothing to the world but an abandoned funhouse.

Even though Connor's military insight was five years behind current events, he would know how to protect the Land from being found by Global or China. Bailey felt the edge of a fingernail to bite as she waited for his response.

Connor paced to the back door and parted the curtains to look outside. Revel and Lydia watched his back, and Justin's head bobbed as he fought to remain conscious.

Slowly, Connor turned to them, making solid eye contact with each person before he knelt in front of Justin. "Mercer, can you hear me? Mercer?"

Justin grunted one note, but kept his eyes closed.

"Was Koslov injured in the landing?"

"I don't know, but everyone in Global has standing orders to kill any defector. That's what I am to them now, so it's his duty to kill me." He slumped again as if speaking had taken the last of his energy. "You have to hide me."

Connor braced him. "Stay with me, Mercer. You never looked like this after a hard landing, and we had several together. What really happened?"

Justin's eyes remained shut. "I approached the Land's outer perimeter at about one hundred feet above sea level. As soon as I flew through the crackly haze, the bluffs appeared directly ahead. I experienced L.T.E. on the beach and had a rollover accident."

Revel lifted a palm. "L.T.E.?"

Connor answered Revel without taking his eyes off Justin. "Loss of tail rotor effectiveness."

Justin continued, "When I hit the sand, the blades flew off, and the doors popped open. My side was facing up. I climbed out and crawled away, then hid while my vision straightened. That's where Bailey found me."

Connor looked back at Bailey. "Did you see the crash?"

She shook her head, recalling the muffled sounds. "I only heard it. I think they hit near the rocks below the bluffs. I couldn't see anything from the cliff, so I ran down. That's when I spotted him hiding in the brush."

Connor raised one eyebrow at her. "Did you see anyone else?"

"No."

He asked Justin. "Was Koslov injured?"

"Probably. He wasn't moving when I got out."

"How bad was the damage to the helicopter?"

"It's destroyed."

"Does Koslov have a radio or phone? Any way of contacting the ship?"

"I don't know. There was no communications equipment on the helicopter—I made sure of that. But he might have a phone with him." Justin opened his eyes again. "All the Russian recruits are allowed secured satellite connectivity, but they haven't been able to get a signal in days."

Connor blew out a breath and stood. "I will go out and get Lydia's medical supplies so she can treat your injuries in here. She's making you gray leaf tea now. You know all about that." He looked at Revel. "After I tell John what's happening, you and I will ride out to tell Levi and Everett, and we'll search for Koslov together. Bailey, stay here with Lydia."

As he lifted the cottage key off a hook by the back door, he glanced at Justin. "Is Koslov armed?"

"Most definitely."

* * *

Revel stood in the doorway between the kitchen and the parlor with his boots on and his coat buttoned. He stretched his neck deep to one side and then the other while Connor was upstairs briefing John on the situation. The clock on the parlor wall read a quarter past three. His body wished he were asleep in bed and his mind was perplexed by all that had happened, but his hands were ready to protect those he loved.

From his position he had a clear view into the kitchen and easy listening to the conversation upstairs. Connor spoke in a hushed but hurried voice to John. Little Andrew's door hadn't opened; thank goodness he'd slept through the chaos.

Every lantern and wall sconce in the kitchen burned at full flame while Lydia treated Justin Mercer's wounds and Sophia assisted her. Revel fixed his gaze on the unwelcomed outsider. The man looked to be only half conscious while the gray leaf medicine spread through his system. Still, Revel stayed ready to strike if he made any threatening movement toward the ladies.

Bailey had left the ladies alone in the kitchen with Mercer and was pacing the parlor rug. She spoke in a barely audible but fully enraged tone. "He shouldn't have come here. I bet every officer on that Global ship is scouring for clues to where Justin went in that helicopter."

Revel glared at the outsider in the kitchen. He didn't want anyone with ill intentions coming to the Land any more than Bailey did, but if Mercer was dangerous, wouldn't she be watching him rather than marching back and forth across the parlor floor?

When Sophia handed a threaded needle to Lydia, Revel couldn't bear to look at the medical scene in the kitchen any longer. He caught Bailey's eye and opened his arms.

It surprised her enough to halt her pacing. She narrowed her defiantly beautiful gaze at him.

That look didn't bother him; he grew up with two sisters.

He kept his arms open and curled his fingers, bidding her to come to his embrace.

Her expression softened, more with humor than with need. "I don't want to hug, Rev. I want to kick his teeth in."

Revel didn't speak but only curled his fingers again.

This time she came.

He wrapped her stiff shoulders in his arms and pressed his cheek to the top of her warm head. "You won't hurt Mr. Mercer. It would only give Lydia more work to do."

"I know." She rested against his chest and let him hold her for a brief moment. Her whisper hid the strength of a roar. "I'll wait and take my frustration out on that Global guy when we find him."

Revel didn't know what he would face—what any of them would face—when they encountered the missing man. Hopefully, they would locate him before he could hurt anyone, especially Bailey. For now she was in his arms, so she was safe.

Before he could speak, she pulled away. He wanted to draw her back in but knew better than to try.

She stared up at the ceiling as if the answers to all her unasked questions were written there. After a moment, she looked back at him. "I want to go with you and Connor to search for him."

"Connor needs you here."

She blew out a breath so hard the short tresses hanging over her forehead flew to the side. "I'll never fit in with this chauvinistic society."

"It's chivalrous."

She groaned. "Whatever."

"There is a difference."

"I can drop any guy in the Land with one punch, and—"

"Except Connor."

"Except Connor. So far." She held up a finger and smirked. "We'll spar again."

"For now he wants you to stay here."

"See. He's a chauvinist."

"No, he is smart."

She cocked her pretty chin, fire burning behind her amber eyes. "You know I can defend myself and protect everyone else if I have to."

"And that is why Connor wants you here. You're his best fighter, so he's leaving you to watch over those he most cherishes—his wife and son."

She closed her mouth, then peered into the kitchen where Lydia was stitching Mercer's face. "I hadn't thought of that."

"Because you expect the worst in people."

The darkness returned to her eyes. "Yeah, with good reason." She raked her fingers through her cropped hair, leaving it in a disheveled pile that was more appealing than any tidy style. "I want to find the Global guy and make sure he doesn't expose the Land to his... comrades."

Sometimes the best way to get through to Bailey was to use her vernacular. He grinned at her and waited until she looked him in the eye before he spoke. "Let me and Connor have some of the fun, okay?"

"Okay." She softly play punched his arm. "Just be careful out there."

"Connor said we are treating this as a search and rescue mission. But it's still Connor, so you know he will be alert. We will be fine." He caught her hand and held it. "You be careful here."

Connor hurried down the stairs, shrugging into the black jacket he'd brought to the Land, faint discoloration the only proof military patches once adorned its sleeves. "John approved my plan." He lifted his chin at Revel. "You're with me."

Revel gave Bailey one last look then followed Connor to the barn. They readied their horses and rode out to Levi's house, then across the dark road to Everett's. Both men answered the door half asleep but still dressed from guard duty, and neither man seemed surprised by Connor's news—only angry that Justin Mercer had returned to the Land.

Connor gave efficient orders. Everett was to alert the men who worked and lived on his farm while Levi rode into the village and spoke to the nearest elder, who would then relay the information to the others. Then, both men would leave their horses at the Colburn house and meet Connor and Revel near the cairn on the shore to begin the search.

As Revel rode beside Connor back to the house, he recalled the sounds that came from the forest when he was looking for Bailey. The breeze chilled his neck, and he scanned the dark brush on either side of the road. The man they were going to search for might be watching them even now.

Revel adjusted the straps across his chest; one held his crossbow on his back, the other held his quiver. He kept his voice as quiet as he could, though loud enough to be heard over the horses' canter. "Earlier, when I was walking outside to find Bailey, I heard rustling along the back of the property. It was coming from the path that leads to the bluffs, but she and Mr. Mercer came out of the forest path from the shore."

The faint glow of first light made Connor's profile shadowy. "What did it sound like to you?"

"Might have been a man, might have been a deer or rabbit."

Connor didn't say anything else as he rode. Was he disappointed in Revel or simply trying to listen for more sounds?

The steady clip-clop of their horses' hooves was the only noise until they neared the Colburn property. Then, the rooster's blaring crow cut through the pre-dawn air. Revel almost cursed the bird while they tied their horses outside by the back door.

After a quick check of what was happening with Mercer in the house, they walked to the forest path. Connor had called this a *search and rescue mission*, but he held his crossbow at his side.

The growing light allowed them to see a few feet into the brush on either side of the path, though not far enough for Revel to feel comfortable. He didn't release a full exhale until they stepped out of the forest near the cairn on the shore.

High tide brought the water too far inland to walk around the boulders to find where Mercer said the helicopter had its hard landing. Revel still wasn't sure what that meant. He doubled his pace to be beside Connor instead of behind him. "What are we looking for exactly?"

"Anything unusual. The small helicopter Mercer was flying broke apart when he crashed. The debris would be under the waves by now, maybe carried out to sea." Connor scanned the ocean from one end of the red horizon to the other. "I don't see any debris out there… or the ship." He pointed at the incline nearby that went up to the bluffs. "I need to get a look from up there. We have time before Levi and Everett arrive. Let's go."

They passed the smattering of footprints in the sand where Bailey found Mercer in the brush and followed the narrow prints of her hiking boots between the boulders and up the grassy steep. Once atop the bluff, Connor withdrew Bailey's binoculars from his jacket pocket and faced the soft light that was growing over the horizon. "Nothing visible on the sea. Good."

Revel toed the cliff's edge. Violent waves crashed over the boulders far below. "I don't see anything down there either."

Connor slid the binoculars back into his pocket. "Let's go back to the cairn to meet Levi and Everett." He took a step then halted, staring at the ground. He lifted a hand for Revel to stop too.

Revel followed his line of sight. Thick reddish splotches dotted the cliff's dirt and rocks. "Blood?"

Connor nodded once and followed the trail of drips from the dirt to the dry grass. A swath of tall grass was flattened in all directions. In the center of the disturbance, a black, hand-sized, rectangular object stuck out of the tussock. Its shiny surface was almost glass-like.

Revel pointed at it.

Connor's wide eyes scanned the area around them as he crouched slowly and picked up the rectangular object. When he touched its reflective surface, it illuminated with numbers and symbols over an image of a smiling blonde woman and two children who resembled her.

Connor tapped the symbols and another image appeared—this one included a man, tall and thick-shouldered with an angular face and a dark marking of a bear on his forearm.

Revel checked the path, the cliff behind them, and the grassy bluff. When he saw no one, he crouched beside Connor. "What is this device?"

"It's a phone."

"What is it used for?"

"Communicating."

"Is it communicating now?"

Connor tapped another symbol on the object's glass surface. "No, but it will tell me what I need to know as soon as I change the language setting from Russian to English."

CHAPTER FIVE

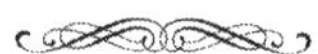

Bailey watched the clock on the wall behind John's armchair in the living room while she tried to ignore the faint snores coming from the sofa. The medicinal gray leaf tea had knocked Justin out cold after Lydia expertly stitched his wounds. The former naval flight officer would probably sleep for hours while the miraculous gray leaf healed his body. He looked like he needed the rest. There had to be more wrong with him than his injuries from the landing.

Justin Mercer might not be graciously welcomed back to Good Springs, but he was the person who introduced Bailey to the Land. Not that she owed him or anything… yet she did. She shook open a crocheted throw blanket and draped it over him while wondering if his mother was still alive back in Virginia.

Metal clinked lightly in the kitchen as Lydia and Sophia sanitized their instruments. Both women were too frightened of the missing Global deckhand to go out to the medical cottage.

Little Andrew was still asleep upstairs, but dawn's rosy light was warming the east-facing windows and would soon wake him. He'd been an infant when Justin was here two years ago, so he wouldn't know the stranger sleeping on the sofa.

Bailey sat in the chair across from John, where she had an ear to the kitchen, an eye on the front door, and Justin within arms' reach in case he suddenly awakened and freaked out. Connor had trusted her to protect his family while his team searched for the Global guy. If only she could be out there with them instead of here beside Lieutenant Snore.

She wouldn't normally care if the gray leaf tea made Justin sleep all day, but he had brought dire news to the Land and the leaders should be told immediately. With Justin in a gray leaf coma, she was the only person who could tell them.

John looked up from his open Bible, his soft voice fatherly. "What troubles you, Bailey?"

If he'd asked her that before two o'clock this morning, she would have told him about the odd discontent that had reverberated in her soul for weeks. It was like there was something she wanted deeply, but couldn't define. It seemed silly now that she was facing genuine problems again, true and dangerous troubles that guaranteed challenge and adventure. In fact, now she couldn't conjure that dissatisfaction at all. Weird.

Though Justin probably wouldn't have roused even if Bailey answered John at the top of her lungs, she kept her voice down. "All of it, I guess."

John gently closed his treasured book and laid it on a side table by a glowing lantern. "Remember in our letters when we talked about the passage from the eighth chapter of Romans?"

Her mind couldn't downshift from action to academic that fast. "Um…"

"Verse twenty-eight? I told you to memorize it."

"Oh, yeah." She closed her eyes while she envisioned the underlined sentence in her Bible. Once the image was clear, she recited the verse. "*And we know that all things work together for good to them that love God, to them who are the called according to His purpose.*"

John nodded approvingly. "You can trust God to work these circumstances for your good just as He has providentially used everything else in your life."

It was hard to argue with that kind of faith, yet her insides fluttered with energized nerves. "It isn't simply Justin's arrival or even having a Russian deckhand on the loose that worries me."

"Then what does?"

She shouldn't be the person giving the overseer of Good Springs the bad news. Justin was supposed to tell Connor, then Connor would think it over and form a survival plan for the Land, and then he would tell John. She had caused enough trouble when she came here a year ago; she didn't want to be the one to announce they would all freeze then starve to death. Or vice versa. It probably didn't matter in what order the atrocities would come on the innocent people of the Land.

But they were coming.

John not only expected a truthful answer from her, he deserved one. She listened for the sounds in the kitchen. Lydia and Sophia were still talking and had started preparing breakfast, so Bailey had a few moments of privacy with John. Still, she lowered her volume. "Justin told me there has been nuclear warfare in the outside world. Nations have been launching their most destructive bombs at each other."

John leaned back in his armchair, his cheeks shiny in the growing dawn light. "Connor told me years ago about the meaning and possibility of nuclear warfare. And the potential aftermath for humankind."

That made her job of explaining this simpler, but no less painful. "It gets worse. Justin said thick upper level ash is now spreading across the globe. It will fill the sky—everywhere, even here. From the ground it will look similar to an approaching storm. Only this cloud won't blow away for a very long time."

John's crystalline eyes darkened in a way Bailey had never seen before. "Connor told me about the theory of nuclear winter. Is that what is happening?"

"This is technically volcanic winter. There were many nuclear blasts, and that might be why the earth's tectonic plates are shifting more than normal. Hundreds of volcanic eruptions have occurred, including multiple dormant super volcanos. Justin said the Global scientists blame the nukes, but I doubt that caused it."

"Hundreds of volcanos are erupting? Where?"

"Mostly around the Pacific Rim. Justin said the particles are so thick in the upper atmosphere that the sunlight isn't expected to be seen through the cloud cover for at least two years. That will mean worldwide devastation. He said that's why he came here… to warn us."

John propped his elbows on his knees and steepled his fingers as he gazed at a sleeping Justin Mercer. John's outward silence left Bailey desperate to know his thoughts. If his resolve to trust God no matter what was faltering, hers would shatter. She had depended on his faith to bolster her own. Now that she knew the strength true Christ followers gave each other, a solitary faith would never suffice.

John didn't take his eyes off Justin for a long while, nor did he speak. Maybe he was praying for him, for them all, for the world. John was like that—instead of praying for himself, praying for people she would consider enemies. Maybe she would be like John someday.

For now, she could only think of how her new and lovely life was about to change. If the sun was completely obscured, tending the greenhouse back at the inn would be pointless. Nothing would grow. Herbs only needed four hours of sunlight, but vegetables needed at least six. It wasn't just her work that would be in vain: the crops wouldn't grow in Isaac's fields. The livestock wouldn't have food, except for any stubborn grass or ground cover they might find.

They were all in for hard times. And not just at Falls Creek, but here in Good Springs and in Woodland and Southpoint and Riverside and all the other villages of the Land.

Just when she thought she was anchored in a peaceful place, her lifeline was about to unravel.

For her, and for everyone.

Revel was happy with his new courier service, and Eva and Sybil were settling into their new marriages. James and Naomi were soon to wed. They were all getting to enjoy the pleasant circumstances for which they'd worked so hard, but now their lives would turn into a struggle to survive.

And that was if the missing deckhand didn't kill them all or expose the Land to a dying world.

She couldn't stop the clouds. However, she could hunt down the Global guy—Sergei Koslov or whatever his name was. She couldn't sit here and worry any longer. Nervous energy propelled her to stand abruptly. John could sit here and pray all he wanted. She had to *do* something.

Just as he looked up at her, the back door opened, and the murmurs of several men flowed from the kitchen and into the living room.

Her racing heart calmed the instant Revel stepped through the doorway. For a fleeting second it felt like everything would be okay. She met him by the staircase, feeling better with every step closer to him. "Did you find the Global guy?"

He gave her arm a light squeeze and shook his head. His eyes were already shadowed and the day had just begun. He stepped aside while Connor and the others came into the living room.

John stood and gave Levi and Everett an acknowledging glance before looking at Connor. "What news?"

Connor held up a phone, and every muscle in Bailey's body tensed.

She hadn't seen such a device from the outside world for a year, and knowing it could be used to expose the Land, she'd hoped to never see one again. "Where did you get that?"

None of the men acknowledged her question. Revel put a gentle hand to her low back and pushed as if to usher her out of the room. She stayed right where she was.

Connor flicked a glance at Revel, and he removed his hand from Bailey.

Though relieved to be allowed to stay without an argument, she missed Revel's touch when it was gone—his warmth, his strength.

What was happening to her?

Connor explained the phone to John while the others watched intently. He tapped the screen and showed John that he'd disabled the phone's ability to send and receive signals. Then he displayed a photo of the man he believed they were looking for and pictures of the man's family.

John sat back down. He leaned his head against the high back of the chair while he scratched his bearded cheek. "This man has a wife and children."

"Yes, sir. It appears so." Connor sat on the edge of the chair across from John as if they were the only two people in the room. "There was a lot of blood in the area where we found this. We followed the blood trail to the edge of the cliff but couldn't see Koslov below. If he went over the cliff, there is no way he would have survived the rocks and the water."

Levi raked his fingers through his sun-kissed brown hair. "But if he is alive, he would be hard to find. You said in the military you were trained in evasion tactics and survival skills. Wouldn't he possess those skills too?"

Before Connor could reply, Everett crossed his arms. "Then he is even more of a threat than we thought."

Bailey nodded her agreement, but no one gave her a blip of attention.

Connor's gaze remained fixed on John. "The man couldn't have survived that descent, especially in his condition."

At Connor's denial of the threat, Bailey swallowed the air in her mouth. Revel returned his hand to her back. He knew what she was thinking without her saying a word, and his touch was the only thing anchoring her to this discussion instead of charging outside to hunt down Koslov.

Levi's tone was more growl than voice. "I alerted the village elders before sunrise. Should we activate the communications network across the Land?"

Revel took a half step forward. "I can ride to the other villages at once to let the overseers know what is happening."

When John didn't respond, Connor glanced back at Revel. "Not yet. When the tide rescinds, we will attempt to recover the body below the bluffs."

Ignoring Connor's opinion, Levi looked to John. "Father, we must find this man immediately before he hurts someone or contacts his people."

Connor shook his head. "If by some miracle the man survived, he would need our help."

Bailey held her breath as the tension between the men crackled through the room. Connor had trained them for years to defend the Land against outsiders. Then he'd experienced a change of heart and decided they should help any newcomer instead of attacking them. Bailey's hand immediately covered the still-numb scar on her outer thigh where they'd shot her when she came ashore last year.

Connor now had a more peaceful approach to the Land's security after years of theological training with John. Bailey should be pleased. If Connor hadn't hyped up his team before she arrived, she wouldn't have a scar and Tim might still be alive. She didn't appreciate Connor's tough cop tactics back then, but now that this beautiful place was her home and its inhabitants her friends, she wanted to protect it too.

Especially from Global.

So, as adamant as Connor was that the missing man was dead, she agreed with Levi and Everett. A Global representative was somewhere out there and should be located at once, even if she had to do it herself.

John folded his hands in front of his chest the way he did during a sermon when he was explaining a difficult Bible passage. He made eye contact with every person in the room except Bailey. "Gentlemen, at present it seems the missing man is injured and hiding, or most likely dead. If he is alive, however, he needs our kindness. We will not fear him. Levi, Everett, go home and eat breakfast. Take care of your families and chores. I will call a meeting of the elders at the chapel at noon. Meanwhile, Connor, you may listen for radio signals on your device in the barn to ensure the missing man isn't in contact with his people. If Mr. Mercer awakens before the meeting, I will ask him for more details." He looked up at Bailey. "On this and other matters that concern us." He returned his gaze to the men. "We will reconvene at the chapel at noon."

As the men obediently filed out of the room, John spoke once more. "Revel, please tend to the barn chores this morning. Connor and Bailey, stay here. I must speak with you both in private."

Connor gave Revel a nod as if telling him it was okay to leave, then he raised one eyebrow at Bailey.

Once the others left, John opened a hand to the side chairs. "Bailey, Connor, have a seat. I'll be back in a moment."

Bailey lowered herself to a chair, but Connor didn't sit. She could feel him watching her, so she looked up at him. "What?"

"I told you not to go to the shore."

"But now you're glad I did, aren't you?" She pointed a thumb at the unconscious man on the sofa. "He would still be curled up in the brush and bleeding if I hadn't gone down there."

"You disobeyed direct orders."

"I'm not under your command, Captain Connor. Besides, you went to the beach during your watch too."

He drew his head back. "No, I didn't."

"I saw the sand on the kitchen floor before I left for my shift."

He gazed at her with puzzled eyes as John came back into the room. The older man patted Connor's shoulder. "Have a seat, son. Bailey has important news from the outside world. You need to hear this."

For once she knew something Connor didn't. Any pleasure she might have taken vanished under the weight of what they were about to discuss.

* * *

Revel unrolled his shirt sleeves and buttoned his cuffs as he hurried from the Colburns' barn to the village chapel. The first day of autumn had warmed quickly, and he'd broken a sweat while mucking out the stalls. But now he needed to look somewhat decent for the village elders' meeting.

He wasn't a resident of Good Springs, and he certainly wasn't an elder here. If he made his home in Falls Creek and the village became large enough to ordain elders, he would be eligible since he was the firstborn son of the founding family.

But he had left Falls Creek.

And he was no leader.

John Colburn invited him to this meeting because the elders preferred to hear firsthand accounts of incidents. Revel had been with Bailey after she found Justin Mercer and with Connor while he searched for the missing man and found the phone device in the grass and the blood trailing over the cliff.

Hopefully, the elders wouldn't question him too much about Mercer's nervous ramblings or about the missing man's whereabouts. Revel had already told John all he knew. It was up to the elders to decide what should be reported to the other villages; his job was to relay those reports while on his courier route.

With all that was going on, he'd almost forgotten he was scheduled to leave Good Springs tomorrow. He still hadn't used the new mailbag he'd received as payment for escorting the McIntosh family to Good Springs. He'd been looking forward to breaking it in and to being on the road again. He enjoyed his courier route across the Land. It ensured he could visit Bailey every few days while she was at the Inn at Falls Creek. He had planned to see her just as often while she was visiting Good Springs. But now that something dangerous was happening, he didn't want to leave her.

There was no one to blame: he had created the courier service himself and won the village overseers' approval for it. He'd planned the delivery route, set the schedule, and worked hard to earn the people's trust—and their reliance. If he was employed by another man and all this was happening, he would resign the job or get himself fired so he could stay and protect Bailey.

But he couldn't fire himself. And he wouldn't disappoint the woman he loved by giving up the business she'd graciously encouraged him to start.

He checked his watch as he took the chapel steps two at a time. He was only a few minutes late. The doors were already closed. So much for making a respectable impression at his first—and probably only—elder meeting.

The men were seated on the first two rows of the chapel. John Colburn stood in front of the lectern; he usually stood behind it when he preached on Sunday mornings. Revel had never seen the overseer wear work clothes in church. His attire matched the rest of the men, who also had left farms and workshops for the impromptu meeting.

Several men glanced back as Revel took the outer aisle toward the front of the chapel. The older gentlemen gave each other inquisitive looks, but Levi and Everett kept stoic expressions. They knew why Revel was attending.

Connor walked out of John's office at the front corner of the chapel. Bailey walked beside him, both of them whispering. Revel hadn't realized she would be here too. Whatever she and Connor had discussed with John during their private meeting this morning had left them all frowning.

Revel stopped halfway to the front and waited to see where Bailey sat. She and Connor broke their quiet conversation as they neared the front row. Connor sat directly in front of John's lectern, and Bailey perched on the far end of the wooden pew, biting the nail of her ring finger.

Most of the elders raised an eyebrow at her simply because a female was present for an elder meeting.

Revel ignored their stares. He pulled off his hat and sat beside her. She switched to another fingernail to bite. He wanted to wrap an arm around her, but refrained. She wouldn't mind that she was the only female at a men's meeting, but she certainly wouldn't appreciate Revel's comfort in front of the others.

John tapped his pencil on the lectern in rapid thumps. "Gentlemen, thank you for breaking from your work to meet. I understand it has been a long day for you since you were awakened before dawn with the news of more outsiders arriving.

"Thus far, we believe there are only two men who made it to the Land during the night: Justin Mercer, whom you will remember from two years ago, and another man. We have not seen the second man. Mr. Mercer said the man's name is Sergei Koslov and he is part of an organization of nations called Global."

John folded his hands as he often did when his sermons deepened. "Both men were wounded when they arrived on the shore early this morning. The aircraft they used was destroyed when it landed. Mr. Mercer is convalescing in my home and is expected to fully recover. We believe the other man's injuries are severe, possibly fatal. Connor and Revel searched for him this morning and found evidence he went over the bluffs. Though we fear he is dead, we will continue to send out search parties throughout the day."

An older man spoke up. "What should we do?"

"Be vigilant and tell your families to be as well."

"Is the man dangerous?"

John turned a palm. “We don’t know. Mr. Mercer says the man is armed. However, we will treat him as a refugee needing our help, unless he proves hostile.” He looked at Connor. “If he somehow survived the fall to the rocks and currents below the bluffs.”

Bailey blew out a long breath and crossed her arms tightly. Whatever she had discussed with John and Connor privately had left her disagreeing publicly. This meeting wasn’t simply about finding Mr. Koslov.

Revel shifted his foot closer to her and gently pressed his lower leg against hers. At his touch she uncrossed her arms but remained as tense as a goat on a fence rail.

John motioned for Connor to join him at the lectern. If he wanted Connor’s account of the morning’s events, this might be when he called on Revel too. Revel wiped his sweaty palms on his pants and watched Connor for a cue.

Connor leaned a casual elbow on the lectern. “Justin Mercer came to the Land to bring us news of catastrophic events happening around the world. Since these events might affect us, he wanted to warn us so that we can prepare.”

“Prepare for what?” one of the elders interrupted.

Connor didn’t acknowledge the impatient man and continued speaking as coolly as if he were telling one of his campfire stories. “The war between the nations has heightened in severity, and the two main belligerents carried out multiple nuclear strikes, mostly around the Pacific Rim. Not only are the blasts immediately destructive but the toxic aftermath will cause more devastation for a very long time.”

The anxious elder raised his voice. “Are we at risk here in the Land?”

"Not from the blasts, as far as we know. But there are now hundreds of volcanic eruptions occurring, and the ash is thickening in the upper atmosphere. The scientists who work for Global claim their enemy's nuclear blasts caused the volcanic eruptions, and vice versa. The cause doesn't matter as much to us in the Land as the effect."

He pointed at Bailey. "Mercer's warning to us is that the increasing ash cloud will block direct sunlight for the whole earth for about two years."

An older man gasped, which made him cough. Other men mumbled to each other, to themselves, to John Colburn.

It was the first time Revel had seen Connor lose a room's attention.

Then as he looked next to him at Bailey, the news sank in: No sunlight for two years.

Bailey met his gaze, her amber eyes sorrowful. She whispered, "Justin told me this morning. I wanted to tell you, but John said not to tell anyone until he and Connor had time to discuss it."

He touched her hand, unable to speak even if he had words to say. It didn't matter when he found out; the outcome would be the same, not only for him but also for everyone here, for his family, for the Land.

No wonder Connor and John didn't seem as concerned about the missing Global man as he expected them to be. One man couldn't cause as much devastation as a two-year winter.

Revel didn't hear what the men around him mumbled, or even when John officially opened the floor for questions. He only leaned back against the hard wooden pew and prayed neither of his sisters were indeed with child.

It was Bailey's hand that squeezed his arm now. Her whisper was as gentle as her touch. "Are you okay, Rev?"

Somehow, he managed a nod and covered her hand with his while the elders peppered Connor and John with questions.

"How cold will it get?"

"What crops might survive?"

"Nothing will grow without sunlight."

"How will we feed our livestock?"

John opened a hand to Bailey. "Gentlemen, that is why I invited Miss Colburn here. She has studied botany extensively and will help us prepare for what might come."

Bailey remained seated but spoke up for the first time in the meeting, her voice crackly with emotion. "The gray leaf tree should be able to survive with low light, as well as some of the groundcover plants, such as clover."

Everett flipped his dark hair off his forehead. "Clover won't sustain my entire flock for two years."

Connor smoothed the air with both hands. "Which is why we must harvest well, and then preserve and conserve."

The men began to mumble again, their concerns overlapping like approaching storm clouds.

"Should we thin the deer herds so they don't overgraze?"

"What's the longest smoked venison will last?"

"Does anyone know how to properly dehydrate milk?"

"Just make cheese blocks and keep them in the cellar. Apparently, it will be cold enough to preserve our food for us."

"Will we have to turn to ocean fishing? I haven't lowered a crab trap in years."

"I haven't been to the fishing shacks south of the village since I was a boy. Are they still standing?"

Their concerns swirled in and out of Revel's ears faster than he could concentrate on any one of them. Then one question came to the front of his mind, and without thinking, he raised his hand. "Will a heavy concentration of ash particles in the atmosphere expose the Land to the outside world?"

Though he could feel all eyes on him, he kept his gaze on Connor. The man he'd looked to for all the answers for over a year simply pressed his lips into a flat line.

John quickly rejoined Connor by the lectern. "Gentlemen, the truth is: we simply do not have the answer. All we have is our determination to work hard, the love of our families, and our faith in a sovereign God. And that is all we need."

He pointed at Revel. "I would like Mr. Roberts to stay with us a few more days before continuing on his courier route. That way, we can prepare our report for the other villages, including Miss Colburn's crop recommendations. Is that agreeable for you, Mr. Roberts?"

"Yes, sir."

"Excellent. Our foremost goal, gentlemen, will be for life in every village to carry on as normally as possible, including the usual harvest celebrations. We want the people to enjoy the fruit of their labor, especially if this is to be the last harvest for a long while."

CHAPTER SIX

By evening, Revel's neck ached. Maybe it was from his lack of sleep, or maybe it was from frequently looking over his shoulder for the outsider whom no one could locate but Mercer claimed would kill him in compliance with their superiors' orders. Connor called the man *Koslov* and said he was dead and no one should worry about him. John called him *the missing man* and said if he was alive, his injuries had probably immobilized him, so he'd ordered another search. Bailey called him *the Global guy* and paced the Colburns' property, ready to choke the life out of every shadow she passed.

If that wasn't enough to make Revel long for simpler days, one village wife after another stopped by the Colburns' to ask for more details about the coming agricultural apocalypse. No one had any details to share because—thanks to the gray leaf medicine—Mercer hadn't awakened from his slumber on the divan in John's parlor.

Revel begged the Lord for sleep that night, but it only came with nightmares.

He rose before the sun, shaved by the early morning light, and then sat at the Colburns' kitchen table after breakfast, staring mindlessly at his coffee cup. Everyone ate in groggy silence, their eyes puffy. No one mentioned Koslov or the coming volcanic ash cloud.

Footsteps shuffled in the parlor, making Revel glance at Connor, and Connor glance at John. Everyone held still and listened for Mercer. The shuffling led to the washroom and then a few minutes later back to the divan.

From where Bailey sat at the end of the table, she was the only person with a clear view into the parlor. She leaned back in her chair and stretched her elegant neck while everyone waited for her report.

A snore came from the parlor, breaking the silence.

Bailey rolled her eyes. Little Andrew giggled. The two of them made silly faces at each other for a moment, Bailey exaggerating her expression every time Andrew laughed.

Revel's heart warmed to see her pause her worries long enough to play with a child.

His enjoyment didn't last as long as the young boy's, for Mercer's snoring grew in volume. At least one adult in the house was able to sleep, even if it was the person who'd brought them trouble.

Revel downed the last of his coffee and waited for it to energize his system. He didn't budge when Bailey and John left the table to wash dishes or when Lydia took little Andrew upstairs for his morning bath. With no mention of the problems at hand, they went about their morning as if all was well.

Everyone except Sophia.

Instead of going directly back to the medical cottage as she did each morning after breakfast, she stood by the door, looking out its window. Her trembling fingers touched the knob, but she didn't turn it.

Connor lifted the coffee pot at Revel and swirled its contents. “You look like you could use the rest of this. Want it?”

Revel shook his head, his mouth too tired to respond.

The snoring in the parlor continued. Mercer might be recovering from his injuries, but twenty-four hours of sleep was more than most men gave to the gray leaf medicine. Most men in the Land, that is.

Well-rested or not, Revel refused to loaf about the Colburn house too. Determination propelled him to his feet, and he marched to the back door. Sophia glanced up at him with worried eyes and withdrew her fingertips from the door knob. He opened it and stepped out into the crisp morning air. After looking in both directions and seeing no sign of anyone, he waved Sophia out.

“Thank you,” she whispered.

He scanned the area in both directions, then escorted her to the cottage and checked the medical office. “It’s quite safe,” he said at regular volume.

If John was able to go about his day as if everything was fine and if Connor could casually sip coffee while one outsider snored in the parlor and another’s whereabouts went unknown, Revel could also live as though all was well.

The women, however, might not be able to muster the natural courage beholden to men. Beholden to most men. Maybe not him, not naturally anyhow.

If courage was natural to men, why was there a nagging voice—whether of his mother or father, he did not know—deep inside his mind that said men must always appear brave, especially for the sake of women?

Now that he thought about it, most of the women in his life possessed the same measure of courage as the men. Especially Bailey. She feared nothing. If only he could say the same for himself.

Not that he quaked in fear at every thunderclap, but it did seem all the brave decisions came from the men around him—from men like John and Connor. In any difficult moment he looked for the nearest brave man to make the decision, to embolden the cause, to take the stand. He simply followed their lead.

Following the brave took little courage. Then again, he didn't live a life that put him in the position to lead. He wasn't an overseer or elder or manager. He was only a courier, and before that a dozen other short-term occupations, all of which kept him free of serious responsibility. Sure, he was responsible for delivering letters and packages in a timely fashion, but that was no more weighty than being responsible for the evening milking.

His work was a child's chore, albeit on a fast horse.

And it was the work he'd chosen so that he might avoid making tough decisions or being responsible for others in the way a village elder or overseer or even a husband was.

Because he lacked courage.

He wasn't brave, and if the voice in the back of his mind was correct and all real men were brave, he wasn't even a real man.

He was a twenty-nine-year-old child.

No wonder Bailey only wanted to be friends with him. How could he ever hope to win the heart of a woman more courageous than himself?

He could not.

So, his choice was simple: either give up his dream of a life with Bailey or become the man she deserved.

Instead of closing Sophia safely in the medical cottage, he turned back to her. “Would you like me to stay here with you while you work?”

She wrung her hands and nodded. “Um, no, you have things to do. I wouldn’t want to trouble you.”

“It’s no trouble, Miss—”

“I got this, Rev.” Bailey’s full American voice came from behind him as she sauntered into the medical office with a stack of books in the crook of her arm. “Sophia and I have research to do. Thanks, though.”

“Very well. I’ll be in the barn if you need me.”

She wouldn’t need him. He backed away from the cottage and watched the door close.

Rosy sun rays broke through the hazy morning clouds. Above them a soft sky awaited its blue. It would be a fine day, and a brave man wouldn’t waste it staring at a closed door. He marched toward the barn to start the chores that John usually assigned him whenever he stayed here: milking the cow, cleaning the stalls, feeding the horses.

Normally on a fine morning, he would let the horses out to spend the day in the paddock. Today, he hesitated at the stall gate holding Blaze’s lead line. He petted the white stripe on his horse’s face. “I don’t know if a wounded Russian Global soldier or sailor or whatever-he-is would steal a horse. I’m not willing to take that risk with you, buddy. Connor says he’s dead. Bailey says he isn’t. Let’s keep you inside, just to be safe.”

He closed the gate, leaving Blaze where he was. As he walked to the oat barrel, the Colburns’ new rooster crowed in the yard behind the barn. Within seconds, all the chickens were flapping, and Blaze starting kneeing his stall gate while rapidly raising and lowering his head.

Revel dropped the scoop in the oat barrel and hurried to the barn door. The morning sun was rising through the trees, casting long shadows across the lawn. He scanned the paddock, the entrance to the forest path at the end of the property, and the back of the medical cottage but saw no one.

Perhaps someone's dog was wandering around, terrorizing the chickens. It seemed unlikely in Good Springs.

The curtains on the medical cottage window parted and Bailey's silhouette appeared in the window. He couldn't see her eyes from this distance. He shrugged in case she was looking at him and had also wondered what the commotion was. The cottage curtains closed.

The animals settled. Neither John nor Connor appeared at the kitchen window.

If no one else was going to be concerned, neither would Revel.

When he turned to go back into the barn, something on the ground caught his eye. It was a frayed piece of school paper, folded in quarters. He unfolded it and read the penciled message written in sloppy letters: *I mean no harm. Give food please.*

* * *

Bailey stepped away from the cottage window to return to the books she and Sophia had spread across the work table in Lydia's office.

Sophia lowered her taut voice. "That man might be out there… watching us. Aren't you going to close the curtains?"

"Yeah, sure." Bailey slid the cotton panels across the curtain rod until their lacy seams touched. "I don't think the Global guy will peep in your windows, though."

Lydia's young assistant smoothed her honey-colored hair until every strand was secured. "Who knows what he is capable of?"

There was nothing Bailey hated more than to see a woman afraid of a man. "I need to teach you a few things."

Sophia tapped a stack of old botany books on the work table. "About plants?"

Bailey almost laughed but tamped down her humor for Sophia's sake. "No. About self-defense."

"Do you mean fighting moves like those Connor teaches the men?"

"Yes, but better. You should know smart ways to defend yourself."

"Oh, I couldn't fight a man."

"That's the point. If you learned how to defend yourself against an attacker, you wouldn't be afraid all the time."

Sophia shook her head rapidly, loosening the hair strands she'd just tucked in. "You are far braver than I am. I'd rather not know how to fight." She lifted her chin. "I prefer to trust God."

"Super. Then you won't mind if I open the curtains."

Sophia's cheeks flushed, but Bailey opened the curtains anyway. The girl wouldn't learn to be brave unless she saw how it worked.

Beyond the window Revel was walking from the barn toward the house. He slipped a piece of paper into his trouser pocket while looking in all directions, probably as worried about the missing Global man as Sophia was. All at once, Bailey forgot about Sophia and their research. She wanted to leave the cottage and go be with Revel, to hear his voice, to receive his smiles.

They had barely spoken since Mercer's arrival. After the elder meeting everyone received an assignment from John, and that was what they'd all focused on doing.

Revel marched solidly to the kitchen door and disappeared inside. Whatever he was assigned to do, he was too busy for conversation. She was supposed to be working too. Her recommendations for cold-weather crops wouldn't write themselves.

She pulled a wooden stool up to the worktable, then opened her notebook and flipped through all the thoughts she'd scribbled down late last night. "Okay, so in my plant biology classes we studied places that remain under near constant cloud cover like the Faroe Islands. They now produce much of their own vegetables with hydroponics and grow lights, but that isn't an option in the Land."

"What do you suggest?"

She tapped the stack of botany journals she'd borrowed from the village library. "Since vegetables grown for their fruit or roots generally require six hours of sunlight per day, we need to also think of all the plants in the Land that are grown for their leaves, stems, or buds. None of them will thrive without some sunlight, but we don't know how thick the ash cloud will be or how long it will last… if it comes at all."

Sophia's round eyes widened. "What do you mean *if it comes*?"

She hadn't mentioned her doubts about Mercer's report to John or Lydia yet, so she certainly wouldn't tell Sophia. She drew columns on a blank page and opened the first journal. "Let's start with roots... Carrots can grow in partial shade. Maybe radishes, beets..."

Sophia looked up from her book. "We could try potatoes."

"We could. And in the *leaves* category, let's see..." She thought while she thumbed through the journal. "I grew spinach and lettuce in the greenhouse last winter at the inn. Look in those texts to see if any villages grow kale or Swiss chard. Without sunlight, the leaves would be thinner but should taste the same."

The cottage door opened and Sophia flinched so abruptly she clapped the dusty book shut.

Bailey gave her a calming pat on the back and looked toward the door. "Hey, Lydia. We were just—"

"I'm sorry to interrupt your work, but Justin is awake. My father and Connor are at the chapel. Justin is asking for you."

"Okay. I'm coming." She slid her notebook over to Sophia. "Go through these botany journals and list all the potential plants and where they are grown in the Land. Note them here. I'll be right back." Even as the words came out of her mouth, she knew she wouldn't be. If Justin wanted to talk to her instead of waiting for Connor, the Global guy really was the biggest threat.

Sophia was probably right to be nervous. Poor girl. She really should learn self-defense.

Bailey passed Lydia at the door and hurried from the cottage to the house. Revel was in the kitchen, lining a basket with a tea towel. She gave him a sidelong glance and affected her voice with a cartoon quality. "Going on a pic-a-nic?"

Revel's lips parted, but he didn't respond. Instead of asking what she meant as he usually did, he simply looked away from her. Maybe he hadn't eaten enough at breakfast, or maybe John was sending him on an all-day errand. Either way, it wasn't her concern. At the moment, getting the truth out of Justin was.

When she stepped into the living room, Justin sat up but kept the quilt over his legs. She pulled John's footstool over to the sofa and sat close enough to look into Justin's eyes. "You look better."

A cocky grin curved his lip and disappeared under his scraggily beard. "Still have feelings for me, don't ya, beautiful?"

"Nope. Never did." She fanned her nose. "Would it kill you to go take a shower?"

"You missed me."

Something dropped in the kitchen. Revel wouldn't understand if he overheard their banter. She lowered her volume as she said to Justin, "You have dried blood in your facial mop."

That slapped the conceit out of his swollen eyes. It was a shame too, as she was ready to fire at him until he was put in his place.

He smoothed his beard, but it didn't help. "Did you find Koslov yet?"

"No. Will he try to kill you?"

"Those are his orders. I figure between Connor and you and Connor's snarling brothers-in-law, I'm safe here." He frowned but the affectation felt forced. "At least until the big freeze comes. Then we will all die."

She wouldn't play his game. "When did the volcanic eruptions start?"

"Last week."

"When Mount St. Helens erupted, ash drifted around the globe within two weeks. Last night you said you came here to the Land to warn us about the coming volcanic winter. You and I both know it took you more than a week to get assigned to a ship in the South Atlantic and then to ghost program its navigation to come to the Land's coordinates on the equinox." She leaned forward to lock his gaze. "What's your angle?"

He shrugged. "There is no angle."

"You didn't come here to warn us to prepare for a long winter."

"A *two-year* long winter."

"Why are you really here?"

When he didn't answer, she studied the already-healing wounds on his face. "Was it for gray leaf medicine? Did you catch some cooties at your last port-of-call—something penicillin wouldn't cure?"

His arrogant grin returned. "Probably, but that's not why I came."

"Then why?"

"I'm honestly here to help. These people saved my life once, and I when I realized they would have no way of knowing what the volcanic ash was when it covers their precious Land, I wanted to repay the favor."

"And save them?"

"That's right, beautiful." His lips straightened again. "And we don't have much time."

* * *

Revel's heart pounded in his chest as he hurried back to the barn with a covered basket tucked under one arm. He didn't know what he would say if someone questioned him. He'd probably clam up like he did when Bailey had made that picnic joke in the kitchen.

One day he'd be able to defend his decisions, but for now he would have to be satisfied with being able to make them on his own. And not just any decisions: strong decisions. Like the ones Connor and John made all the time.

Finally, he had the chance to take the reins on an important matter. It had taken all his strength not to run to Connor with the note the outsider had left. He had to be able to handle this himself if he was going to be a man worthy of Bailey's affection.

He scanned the barn and the paddock beyond. No one was in sight, so he slipped around the other side of the barn and set the food basket on the ground. He knelt beside the food he hoped would comfort and sustain the stranger and also enable a truce between the man and Mercer.

In the barn's shadow and hidden from view of the house or medical cottage, he wrote a message on the stranger's paper. Knowing the man wasn't a born English speaker, he kept it simple: *We can help you.*

He tucked the paper into a fold of the tea towel that covered the basket and backed away. The stranger was somewhere close by. In the military Connor had been well trained for evasion and survival. Revel didn't doubt Koslov had the same abilities. The man must be healing from his injuries or he wouldn't have been able to sneak to the barn and leave that note in daylight.

No matter where the man was from or what he believed was his duty, his fortitude was admirable. And hopefully, after Revel gained the man's trust and brought him safely into their fold, Bailey—and everyone—would see that Revel was a strong man who could fix problems, protect everyone, and bring the stability to Bailey's life that her fighting spirit never would.

CHAPTER SEVEN

Heavy rain showers pelted the Land on and off for two days, pausing all search efforts, which pleased Revel. He feared for Koslov's health, but wanted to be—needed to be—the person who peaceably introduced the stranger to the community, no matter how the guilt of selfishness ate at him for his secrecy.

After an evening meal of Lydia's chicken casserole, John's freshly baked bread, and Sophia's cinnamon apples, the rains finally stopped and the oval moon peeked down between puffy passing clouds. Revel lingered in the Colburns' kitchen until only he and John were left. The patriarch of the house always sat at the kitchen table on Saturday evenings with an open Bible and looked over his notes for the next morning's sermon.

Revel stepped to the table. "Pardon me for interrupting your studies, Mr. Colburn," Revel pointed to the linen closet, which had a shelf of old clothing and fabric scraps, "but may I rummage through the rag pile?"

"Help yourself. You will find it more plentiful since your last visit. Some the church families donated gently used clothing as we often host travelers in need." He scratched his graying beard and gave Revel a quick head-to-toe scan. "You might find something that fits."

He almost told John the clothes weren't for him but held his tongue and opened the linen closet. Since he had yet to see Koslov, he didn't know what size clothes the man would need. While he picked through the shelves of neatly folded clothing, John left the table and shuffled across the parlor toward the washroom.

Most of the items were for children, but the bottom shelf had a stack of men's clothing. Revel stuffed a blue, button-front shirt, a pair of slightly frayed trousers, and a bundle of wool socks into his new leather mailbag. The bag's stiff leather cover needed to be broken in. It would have its chance as soon as he was back to riding his courier route tomorrow.

How he missed riding Blaze across the Land!

He adjusted the bag's strap and slung it over his shoulder, then set the kettle on the stove to boil. While he waited, he looked out the back door's window. The lamps were burning brightly in Lydia's medical office, creating a soft, orange glow on the closed curtains. Bailey had said she would be working late tonight on her gray leaf research with Lydia and Sophia. The three women had chatted all through dinner about molecules and decay rates and other science details he didn't understand.

John still hadn't returned to his Bible and notebook on the kitchen table. Connor was upstairs with little Andrew, and Justin Mercer was either sleeping or hiding in the upstairs bedroom John had assigned him.

The kettle finally whistled, and Revel yanked it off the stove to silence it. He poured the boiling water into a flask, selected an old cup from the back of the cupboard, and slid both items into his mailbag.

Hopefully, no one would see him.

Dusk settled over the Colburn property as he slipped past the white medical cottage, through the yard, and around to the back side of the barn.

The damp grass sloshed under his feet. He dared not imagine how Koslov fared in the downpours if his hiding place hadn't been well covered. Connor believed the foreigner had fallen from the bluff while injured and the changing tide trapped him in the caves below and killed him, then swept his remains out to sea with the helicopter debris.

Connor was adamant in his theory and said the fact that there had been no sign of the man during their searches since that first morning was proof. The rescue mission turned into a recovery mission, and at dinner this evening, John said it was time for the men to return to their normal routines.

Behind the barn, the full basket Revel had left under the barn's back eave at midday was now empty, as it had been after each meal for the past two days. He rolled the clothes and tucked them into the basket along with the flask and cup and a tea strainer already filled with dried gray leaves. He wedged a note containing carefully written instructions between the flask of hot water and the cup.

As he returned to the house unnoticed, he prayed Koslov would follow the instructions to make the gray leaf tea and drink it to heal his wounds. If Revel knew anything, it was that this was the right thing to do, even if it meant keeping secrets for now.

Though it was his last night at the Colburns' before he had to ride to the southern villages, Revel slept longer and harder than he expected. Somehow, by simply leaving the stranger food, clothing, and medicine, he wasn't worried for everyone's safety any longer. He believed Koslov's message that said he meant no harm, for if he had meant to harm them, he surely would have by now.

After a quick breakfast, Revel hurried to the barn to ready Blaze for the day's ride while the rest of the household prepared to leave for church. Normally, he wouldn't leave the village on a Sunday, but John insisted the urgency of the situation required it.

Revel didn't mind, and since he had missed being on the road, his horse probably had too.

It was a fine day to ride—cool enough from the rains to keep them comfortable, yet not cold enough to weaken their muscles. Without a cloud in the sky, the bright sun would light their path through the gray leaf forest. The chill in the dry autumn air proved changing weather was coming.

According to Mercer, there would soon be a terrible freeze.

And thus Revel needed to be swift on this journey to the southern villages before returning here for a short rest and then riding to the northern villages.

After he led Blaze outside to brush and saddle him in the soft morning light, he left his horse's line looped to the post and walked around to the back side of the barn. He scanned the property as far as he could see and then checked the basket. The clothing and food were already gone, as were the cup and flask, but the gray leaf tea was in its strainer, unused.

The stranger still didn't trust him.

Revel lifted the basket to put it and the tea strainer away in the kitchen. Maybe he was wrong to help Koslov on his own. Now he had to leave the village and wouldn't be able to sneak the man food. He'd done all he could to help the stranger while keeping him far from the house as to not alarm everyone.

Maybe he should tell Connor or John or Bailey.

No. John would want to leave the kitchen door open for the stranger, and though Koslov was a man in need, Mercer claimed the man would try to kill him. Connor would take over what Revel had started, and he desperately needed to be the lead on something in his life. And Bailey still believed the man was a danger. She might use the charity as a trap.

No, Revel should tell no one. He didn't believe Koslov was a threat to their safety, and even though the man was injured, he was taking care of himself out there somehow, so he wouldn't starve while Revel was traveling.

Revel would ride fast and return to Good Springs in a few days and would continue to build trust with the stranger then. It was best for everyone if he kept this situation between him and Koslov for now. This was his chance to be the man Bailey deserved, the man his father would be proud of, the man God was calling him to be.

As he left the barn, the chickens dashed to the other side of their long, narrow coop. He carried the basket to their laying box and lifted its lid. Good—no one had taken the eggs out this morning. It would give him a reason to carry the basket into the kitchen. He nestled the eggs in the bottom of the basket and hurried to the house.

Lydia was standing at the sink, washing Andrew's food-covered fingers in the running water. Bailey was drying dishes and stacking them on the cupboard shelves. She hadn't changed into her Sunday dress yet. Though she didn't enjoy wearing their traditional clothing, he enjoyed seeing her dressed like a woman of the Land.

He set the basket on the countertop. "I brought the eggs in."

Lydia didn't look away from Andrew's hands. "Thank you, Revel."

He left the kitchen before Bailey could ask anything that might require a response. He wouldn't lie about Koslov, but he wouldn't offer any information either. As he turned down the hallway toward the guest room so he could collect his bags and *hit the road*, as Bailey always phrased it, he remembered the prepared gray leaf medicine he'd left beneath the cloth in the basket.

If he returned to the kitchen now and tried to get the tea strainer, empty it, and put it away, the women would ask all the right questions and trap him.

He had two sisters; he knew how that worked.

The only option was to grab his bags and leave the house hastily. Perhaps after a long day at church and lunch at the Fosters', whoever emptied the basket wouldn't think anything of finding the tea strainer, especially with Mercer staying in the house.

Revel slung his new mailbag over one shoulder and his broken-in satchel over the other, then he slapped on his riding hat and gave the comfortable guest room one last check. He would miss the firm bed and the warm quilt while he was sleeping in a tent between villages, but as Connor always said: the mission is more important than comfort. If Mercer was telling the truth that they needed to prepare for a two-year winter, this courier route might be the most important mission of Revel's life.

* * *

Bailey brushed bits of hay from her skirt's hem while John's open wagon came to a stop on the road in front of the Colburn property. She stood from her hay bale seat, remembering the comfort of driving an air-conditioned car. Connor, who was also sitting in the back, lowered the wagon gate for her. She hopped down and stepped to the side of the gravel road. Looking up at John and Lydia, who sat on the front bench, she shielded her eyes from the midday sun. "Enjoy your lunch at the Fosters' farm."

The sun brightened John's crystal blue eyes. "Are you certain you do not wish to come with us?"

Lydia leaned forward to see around little Andrew, who was standing on the bench even though he'd been told twice to sit. "We can wait for you to change your clothes if that would make you more comfortable."

Bailey pulled at the thick fabric collar of her Sunday dress. During the past year, she had trained her mouth not to reveal her dislike of the Land's traditional women's clothing, but her constant fidgeting usually betrayed her feelings. "Next Sunday I will definitely take you up on that offer." She glanced down the driveway at the brick house. "But for today, I think I should stay here."

John tipped his round-brimmed hat and clicked at the horses. Lydia forced Andrew to sit as they started rolling again. Connor popped a long stem of hay into his mouth like a country boy and wiggled his eyebrows at Bailey. "See ya later, Jeans."

"Later." She waved a disinterested hand and marched to the house to get out of the cumbersome dress. Sometimes she wished she'd never made that deal with Lydia a year ago. It almost wasn't worth the stacks of comfortably tailored shirts and pants she'd received in exchange for agreeing to wear a dress to church on Sundays.

But the Land was her home now, and she enjoyed being treated like a respectable woman. When she'd first come here and was introduced to their vintage values, she thought the distinction in gender roles would diminish her value as a person. In the past year, she'd found the truth to be more shocking. They honored women and treasured the differences in the sexes. John said the differences made the combination complete.

Sure, there was the occasional man who only wore good manners like a mask, but there were people like that in every society, in every era. But mostly, the men here respected women simply for being women, mostly because their fathers had raised them to respect their mothers.

And so she'd come to terms with feeling like her Sunday dress was a costume. Lydia had first asked her to wear a dress to church so her appearance wouldn't be a distraction during the service. But over the past year, Bailey's reasons had become more personal. Now, she wore a dress to church to honor them—neither the men nor the women, but the culture as a whole.

She opened the kitchen door, wishing Revel were still here, and there at the stove stood the one man she didn't want to see her in a dress.

Justin disgusted her with a once over look and a long, approving wolf whistle.

She left the back door open and charged straight through the kitchen. "Knock it off. I'm going to change clothes."

He draped a tea towel over his head like a bonnet and faked a female voice. "No, please do keep on your lovely dress. I was just making a spot of tea. How I hoped we could chat about sewing and baking and all the cute plowboys."

She ignored him and locked herself in her room while she put on her jeans and a plain button-front blouse Claudia had made for her at the inn. When she returned to the kitchen, Justin was sitting in John's chair at the head of the table, eating a sandwich as mannerly as a vulture eating roadkill.

"And here I thought I would have to make your lunch and take it up to your sick bed."

He bit off a hunk of the sandwich and didn't bother to chew before he spoke. "I can take care of myself."

"Good. You'll need to because John Colburn won't let you lounge around here once you've fully recovered."

Justin went still. "Did he say that?"

"No, but in the Land if you don't work, you don't eat." She wrapped the rest of the bread loaf Justin had left out on the countertop. "And Lydia won't put up with you leaving a mess in her kitchen."

He shrugged and took another monstrous bite. His broken nose had healed, and most of the bruising was gone, except for dark shadowing under his eyes. Still, he didn't look like his old self. She turned away to make herself a salad. "At least you shaved your stupid face."

"There's my sweet girl."

She wouldn't verbally spar with him. He would enjoy it too much, and she had real questions. "John called off the search for your buddy. Connor says he's dead and swept out to sea."

Justin's eye widened. "He isn't my buddy, and he is still alive."

"Why do you think so? No one can find a sign of him anywhere."

"Global never dies."

She didn't like them either, but his melodrama made her roll her eyes. "Global will be stopped somehow, someday."

When he didn't respond, she plunked her salad plate on the table and sat across from him. "So where is this big freeze you came to warn us about? There isn't a cloud in the sky again today."

"Oh, it's coming."

"It should be here by now."

He swallowed his last bite and leaned back in his chair, leveling his gaze on her. "You're wasting your time by watching the sky. Have you considered that if the gray leaf molecules help hide the Land and if the trees die or go dormant in the big freeze, the Land might be exposed?"

She'd more than considered it. "That is the question behind my research this week. Sophia and I will run experiments to see how the gray leaf might react to a two-year winter. And how we can force molecular release later if we need to. But I don't think that will be our biggest problem."

"Oh?"

"No, I suspect the magnitude of the devastation was concocted by Global for political leverage and to control their population."

Justin swirled the water in his cup and pursed his lips at her. "Always the conspiracy theorist."

Now it was her turn to play his game. If she went quiet and let him do the talking, maybe he would tell the truth. She jabbed the shreds of lettuce, chunks of apple, and crushed walnuts with her fork and swirled them in the vinegar dressing Lydia called a secret family recipe. She chewed slowly and returned her attention to her plate for each bite, not caring if he watched her.

He propped his elbows on the table and laced his fingers together. “Koslov is biding his time. He knows they have been searching for him. He isn’t stupid.”

“Connor and Revel found a blood trail that went over the cliff. The guys all think he is dead.”

Justin looked toward the window. “Koslov isn’t dead.”

She laid her fork across her empty plate and waited for him to return his gaze to her. “So, what do you think I should be doing? Should I be out there hunting down the Global guy or should I be in the lab trying to grow food without sunlight for twelve hundred people next year? Because I can’t do both.”

“It looks to me like you have to do both.” He unlaced his fingers and leaned forward. “If Connor doesn’t think Koslov is a threat and yet you know he is, and if the people here don’t know to manage their food supply for what’s coming but you do, you will have to handle it. It’s all on you, beautiful.”

She ignored what he called her, but the rest of his words hit her gut harder than a roundhouse kick.

It was all on her.

CHAPTER EIGHT

Revel let Blaze carry him across the Land as fast as the horse wanted to travel. Fine weather afforded pleasant roads, and Blaze kept a steady running walk from Good Springs to Woodland, and then from Woodland to Falls Creek. Blaze seemed to sense the urgency of the messages in his master's mailbag.

Revel crossed the stone bridge and rode onto his family's property just after a golden sunset. He scanned the fading sky while he walked Blaze to the long, L-shaped stable block. A flock of geese flew high above, all honking as if the winter approached faster than they could flee. Orange light slipped from the western sky, silhouetting the trees that dotted the pasture all the way to the creek. It was hard to believe a worldwide ash cloud would soon smudge the Land's picturesque sky.

He groomed Blaze in the stable block, then led the horse to his stall and scooped sweet-scented oats into the feeder box. Revel thanked God for another safe day of riding and said good night to the horse he trusted more than most people. "Good job today, Blaze. Sleep well, buddy. We will leave for Riverside first thing in the morning."

He smoothed the white velvety stripe that started between Blaze's brown ears and ended above his nose. "The sooner we deliver the message to all the overseers, the better they can prepare their villages for what might come. But don't you worry, old friend. I'll make sure you stay warm and fed no matter how long the winter lasts."

Blaze smacked his oat-covered lips and lowered his head into the bucket for more.

"Fair enough, buddy." Revel unhooked the lantern from the rough-hewn wall and trudged through the stable block under the weight of his mailbags, satchel, and knapsack. His legs and back grumbled from two days of riding with too few breaks.

Dusk settled over the inn and quieted the property with the promise of rest, save for one anxious rooster who reminded Revel of the Colburns' chickens. Perhaps it had been Koslov sneaking about the Colburn property that had made the fowl restless.

Revel scanned this familiar property; no strangers here but himself. At least that was how it often felt even though Falls Creek was his home.

The last hint of twilight cast a glow across the two-story inn's white clapboard, giving it a lavender tint. Lights burned brightly inside the crowded dining hall's high windows. Inside, his family members ate with the inn's guests—some he knew, some he couldn't recognize from across the yard. Before going into the inn, he carried his bags to the bunk house and deposited them on the only unclaimed bunk.

His back begged for a hot bath as he lumbered across the property to the inn. Blaze seemed to be faring the hasty journey better than he was. Maybe after this trip to the southern villages, he would stay an extra day or two at the Colburns' before heading to the northern villages.

For his horse's sake, of course.

It certainly wasn't because he missed Bailey and couldn't stand the feeling of being apart from her when there was so much uncertainty in Good Springs. He almost chuckled at the lies he told himself.

He glanced back at the stable block before rounding the inn to climb the side steps. If he left here at dawn, he could make his delivery to the Riverside overseer and board a trader's boat for Southpoint by evening.

The back door opened smoother than it had in years. Someone was keeping the hinges oiled. The floorboards in the hallway were freshly waxed, and the wall sconces shone with polished brilliance. Between Falls Creek's new residents—Solo, Isaac, and Naomi—the old house pulsed with new life.

But one thing had not changed.

The air inside the inn was thick with the savory aroma of his little sister's cooking. Revel's favorite part about coming home was still the same, thank God.

He peeked into the kitchen doorway, the scent of roasted venison tempting his empty stomach. Sybil was standing over the double-basin sink, fanning air down her lace collar, sweaty curls clinging to her face.

He shuffled into the warm kitchen. "Are you all right, Syb?"

She turned swiftly, her face flushed and her expression sour. "Oh, Revel! You're here. I would hug you, but I'm in poor form at the moment."

"It is stuffy in here."

A faint smile dimpled her rosy cheeks. "It's more than the heat, I believe, that has me in such a state."

"Are you ill?"

She shook her head and pressed her hand to her middle. At first he thought it might be some female complaint, but his sisters never discussed those issues with him, and he preferred to keep it that way. But then light sparkled in her green eyes, hinting at her blessed secret.

He lowered his bags to the floor. "Sybil! That's wonderful."

"Shh." She touched her finger to her smiling lips. "I want to be sure before I tell Isaac, so don't mention this to anyone. I was waiting for all the signs to be certain."

The mysteries of womanhood were best kept mysteries as far as he was concerned. "I won't tell a soul, I promise."

He bent down to hug her, and her smile vanished. "Oh, dear! Excuse me, please." She put her hand over her mouth and dashed out of the room.

He wouldn't have to keep her secret for long, for surely Isaac had noticed his wife was suddenly indisposed.

The washroom door slammed shut behind her before Revel passed it on his way into the dining hall. Eva was filling water glasses at the guests' tables. She looked every bit the part of a savvy business manager, her clothes smart and her hair smoothly controlled in a tight bun. When their father died, he had bequeathed the inn to Eva and her husband, Solo, but this place had always been hers.

Her gaze roamed the room, constantly making sure all the guests had what they needed. As Revel stepped into the room, Eva immediately spotted him and gave him the same mischievous grin she did when they were children.

She set her pitcher on the nearest table and leaned toward the men sitting there. “Kill the fatted calf boys! Our prodigal has returned.”

The guests laughed, some knowing Revel’s nomadic lifestyle, some not but laughing along with the jovial crowd.

Revel didn’t care. He’d made peace with his desire to travel instead of settle down, and his father had accepted his choice too. Returning to the inn was now simply about visiting the people he loved—his sisters and their husbands and his nephew, who was his favorite kid in the world.

And most of all Bailey when she was here.

Zeke sprang from his seat the way a seven-year-old could, and ran between the tables, one fist still clutching a half-eaten bread roll. “Uncle Revel!” He furled his arms around Revel’s waist. “What did you bring me?”

Revel reached into his coat pocket and withdrew a packet of Adeline McIntosh’s famous rock candy. “Save it for after dinner so you don’t get me into trouble with your mother.”

“I will!” Zeke smiled a missing-toothed grin. “Look, I have two more big teeth coming in!”

“Good for you! Yes, but you seem to have misplaced two more little ones.”

Zeke giggled. “I didn’t misplace them, Uncle Revel. There in a jar in my room.” He ran back to his seat, his little dog close to his heels.

Eva wiped her hands on her apron then kissed Revel’s cheek. “What did you bring me?”

“A few letters and an important message from Good Springs, but that can wait until after dinner.”

"You're right, it can." She lifted her water pitcher from a guest table and winked. "Make yourself a plate in the kitchen and pull up a chair by Zeke."

He gladly obeyed his sister.

As he was chewing his last bite of roast and wishing for more, Sybil finally joined the family at the back table, which was two tables pushed together to form one long table to accommodate the growing herd. His youngest sister gave him a weary look as she sat beside her husband, Isaac.

Revel nodded once at her and glanced at Isaac and back, hoping she got his meaning.

"Now?" she mouthed.

He nodded again. If he knew, the baby's father certainly should know.

She nodded back, then tugged on Isaac's sleeve and whispered to him.

Isaac's eyes widened as he slowly turned his face to her. Revel couldn't hear their whispers over rumblings of the dining hall, but soon Isaac's volume grew along with his smile. "Can we tell everyone?"

"Not yet. Just to be safe."

"All right." He kissed her twice, then pulled her to his side and kept his arm around her while beaming. "Whatever you say, my love. Anything for you."

Fortunately for Sybil, no one else saw the exchange. Eva and Solo were immersed in conversation with Leonard and Claudia, and Zeke was halfway under the table, feeding scraps to his dog.

Isaac carried on as if nothing had changed, but his unfading smile made him look half-crazy while he attempted a normal conversation. "So, Revel, how is Bailey enjoying her time in Good Springs?"

All that had happened since the equinox raced through Revel's mind. He kept his voice steady as not to alarm Sybil while he spoke to the still-smiling Isaac. "Bailey is… keeping busy. There is a matter I must speak to you and Solo about after dinner." He glanced at a nearby table and remembered that Falls Creek now had an overseer. "And to Philip too, of course."

Sybil's dimples flattened. "Is Bailey all right?"

"She's fine, I'm sure."

"You don't sound so sure."

Sybil's tone of voice got Eva's attention. She and Solo gazed at Revel, along with Leonard and Claudia. Even little Zeke paused with his fork halfway to his mouth.

Revel forced a grin. "There is much to discuss, but now is not the time. We can talk after dinner." He tousled Zeke's already messy hair. "It's just boring grown-up stuff. Nothing to concern you."

Zeke gobbled the roast from his fork and returned his attention to his begging dog.

Revel looked away from the concerned eyes of his family and took a long drink from his water cup, having no confidence in his ability to keep a neutral expression if his mouth wasn't busy. In his peripheral vision he could see them all pass worried glances to each other. But then, in one swift motion Zeke sprung to attention and grabbed Revel's arm. "Have you seen the missing fellow?"

Revel swallowed hard. How could the child possibly know about Koslov? He couldn't lie, so he didn't answer but simply looked at Eva. It was a childish habit to want his strong sister's help.

She took his look as a request for more information. "The traders are keeping an eye out for a young man from Riverside who ran away from home. Teddy Vestal is his name. He's done this before and manages to take care of himself, so his parents weren't worried about him at first. But it's almost been three weeks now. This is the longest he's gone without returning home. He's not yet fourteen."

Revel too had dreamed of running away from the inn at that age. He instantly recalled how he felt as a thirteen-year-old, always hiding an unending ache to escape the place where he'd long been loved but once been traumatized. His dry voice betrayed his angst. "Why did the boy run away?"

The change in Eva's eyes acknowledged Revel's past, but she kept her tone light. "His parents say he is hungry for adventure." She pointed her fork at Zeke. "But don't you get any ideas, young man!"

Zeke's eyes widened. "Oh, I won't leave you, Mama. I'd miss the horses and my room and Aunt Sybil's cooking too much." He peeked under the table at his dog. "And you too, Joshua!"

While the adults chuckled and Zeke continued to list his reasons to never leave Falls Creek, Revel stared at his plate and let his vision blur. It wasn't the runaway boy that concerned him but the missing man in Good Springs. Koslov couldn't return to his family when he had enough of his adventure. He was stuck on an island that was hidden to the rest of the world. He was without proper shelter, and now that Revel had left Good Springs, he was without food.

Revel's full stomach soured. He should have told John and the others about his contact with Koslov. Connor believed the man was dead and had given up the search. Justin Mercer believed the man would kill him and was encouraging Bailey to remain defensive. Only Revel knew what the others did not: Koslov was alive and he was no threat. He was simply lost, injured, and hungry.

If Revel's choice ended up causing Koslov's death, he would never forgive himself. It would be the third time in his life he'd felt that type of gripping guilt—first with Charlie Owens hanging himself in the inn's upstairs washroom when Revel was a young man, and then last year when he shot first at Bailey's group when they came ashore.

Why did he keep doing this? How did other men seem to effortlessly make choices and no one died, yet when he thought he was doing the right thing someone lost their life?

Why couldn't he be like other men?

At some point, Isaac and Solo started talking about crops and horses, Zeke took his dog outside, and the girls started clearing dishes. After the guests had dispersed to their rooms, Revel helped move the dining hall tables and chairs while Naomi mopped the worn wooden floor. The letter he'd brought from James was sticking out of her apron pocket, still unopened. If he and Bailey were courting but lived in different villages and he received a letter from her, he would read it at once.

He pointed at Naomi's pocket. "If you want to go somewhere private to read that, I'll finish up here for you."

Naomi kept mopping, her thin arms sinuous from long days of physically demanding work. "Thank you, but I like to wait until I'm settled for the evening to read my mail."

"I'm sure it only says nice things. When Everett brought it to me from the field for James, he mentioned how much James misses you."

Her mop stilled and hunger filled her eyes. "What else did he say about James?"

Revel tried to think back through the chaotic days in Good Springs. "James is looking forward to coming here to you as soon as he drives the flock back from the western pastures."

"Anything else?"

"I don't want to speak for my brother. Maybe you should just read his letter."

A sheepish grin curved her pink lips. He could see why his brother liked her. Everyone had someone to love but him.

He could love Bailey with all of his heart, but as long as she only wanted friendship, he would be but half a man.

When Isaac and Solo finished their evening chores, they met Revel on the front porch. The evening air had cooled pleasantly, and the crickets sang slowly, their summer song over and the silence of winter soon to come. If only the crickets could give the news of the coming freeze, and spare Revel the grief of disappointing his family… again.

Philip crossed the road from the parsonage and joined them on the inn's porch. Falls Creek's new overseer cleaned his spectacles with his sleeve, then looked over the papers Bailey had painstakingly prepared. "This is grim news, indeed, gentlemen." He held the papers out to Isaac. "Plenty of crop information. Perhaps we should make a copy to keep here."

Revel held up a hand. "No need. Bailey sent a copy for each village. Keep that so you can each read it in detail." He thought back to John's directive. "Above all, John Colburn says we must carry on like normal, trust God for our protection and provision, and not let our minds get carried away."

Solo rubbed the scar that divided his eyebrow. "But this cloud cover is not coming here for certain, correct?"

"Correct. We only have the report from the outsider, Justin Mercer."

"Who has proven to be untrustworthy in the past."

"That's right."

Solo shrugged. "Well then, I'll believe it when I see it."

Isaac scanned the papers. "We already harvest and store and preserve using most of these methods anyway."

Philip nodded. "I agree with John Colburn. We should let everyone know there is the possibility of a long winter ahead and to prepare accordingly, but we must not allow a change in circumstance to shake our faith."

Solo slipped his hands into his pockets. "It's settled then. We will follow Bailey's suggestions for the crops, trust God, and not let the ladies get into tizzies about the possibility of a two-year winter. Fair enough?"

Isaac handed the papers back to Philip. "Fair enough."

Revel took a step back, astounded at the difference in the reaction here compared to the tension that prevailed when the news was announced at the elder meeting in Good Springs. Maybe it was Falls Creek's distance from the problem; maybe it was the fact that they hadn't dealt with outsiders crash landing near their homes.

Still, Revel preferred the casual attitude here and wanted to go get Bailey right now and bring her back to Falls Creek forever. Prepare, trust God, stay calm. That felt right. He looked at Philip then at his brothers-in-law and repeated their sentiment. “Fair enough.”

CHAPTER NINE

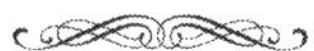

Bailey carted a load of wet laundry to the clothesline in the Colburns' back yard. John followed with a heavy basket of freshly washed towels. Little Andrew toddled behind his grandpa with two eager fists clutching wooden clothespins. He held them up to Bailey. "I help too!"

"Awesome." She plucked the item on top of her clean laundry pile. "We'll start with this wet shirt, okay?"

While she held Connor's white t-shirt to the line, John hoisted Andrew up to pin it in place. The boy's little fingers couldn't work the stiff wooden pegs very well. Bailey almost lost patience and did it for him, but John held him steady. "Keep trying, son."

Finally the peg slipped over the shirt and rope. "I did it!" Andrew beamed as John lowered him to the ground.

"You sure did!" Bailey held out her hand for a high-five. "Good job!"

Andrew smacked her palm just as Connor had taught him. Then he smacked the old t-shirt with both hands. "Daddy's!"

"Yes, that is your daddy's shirt." Bailey continued pinning the clean laundry to the line.

John held another clothespin out to his grandson, but the boy spotted their orange tabby cat prowling over by the cottage and ran to play with it.

Bailey liked Andrew—as far as kids went—but she always felt awkward trying to entertain little ones. Besides, she'd come to Good Springs with a haunting question, and a two-year-old wouldn't have the answer.

With all that had happened on the equinox, she hadn't found a chance to speak to John alone, especially about anything other than ash clouds and Justin Mercer and the missing Global guy. Now that she had a chance, she wasn't sure what to say. She wanted to find an intelligent way to define her question, but all she could think was how much she missed Revel. She lifted her face to the cloudless sky. "It's been a week since the last rainfall."

John pinned a wet towel to the clothesline parallel to hers. "And almost a week since Revel left."

She could feel his knowing gaze on her, so she kept her eyes on her work. "That too."

John added two more towels to the line before he spoke again. "The Lord gives us what we need when we need it."

Were her feelings for Revel changing, and if so, had they become obvious to John? She stared at the pins as she secured her only good pair of jeans to the line. "What we need?"

John didn't respond until she looked at him. Then he simply pointed to the sky. "The Lord will send more rain when we need it."

"Oh!" She chuckled. "Right. The rain."

"And whatever else we need as well." His eyes were bluer than the sky and filled with wisdom. "*Two are better than one...*"

She continued the verse from Ecclesiastes. "*Because they have a good reward for their labor.*"

"Do you know the next verse?"

She shook her head, wishing she'd memorized more of the verses he'd recommended in his letters.

John recited it in the fatherly voice she'd missed hearing. "*For if they fall, the one will lift up his fellow: but woe to him that is alone when he falls.*"

As much as she wanted to claim ignorance of why he quoted that Bible passage, she remembered the panic of being yanked by a vine to the mountain's edge last year, and the peace of knowing she had been safely held in Revel's grip. She nodded as she pinned a pair of socks to the line. "Do you think Revel and I belong together? That the two of us together are better than either of us apart?"

He folded the end of a towel over the clothesline and pinned it securely. "I have witnessed both you and Revel mature over the past year—individually and with each other. If you are asking for my blessing to marry, you would certainly have it. Marriage is indeed God's greatest temporal blessing to mankind. Children are the second. Anytime a godly man and woman have the opportunity to enjoy those blessings, I encourage them." He tilted his chin. "But what I think about your relationship with Revel does not matter as much as what you think."

"I don't know what to think right now. I never thought I would need to consider this at all. So many concepts that are normal to you in the Land are new to me." She stepped back from the laundry baskets. "I love my life here and my work in the greenhouse at the inn and the people. It's everything I could have ever hoped for and more. But the more I settle into my new life in the

Land, the more I feel like there is something missing." Her fingertips tapped her sternum. "It's like there is a question in my heart that nothing will answer. I pray about it constantly, but no answer comes."

John stepped around the baskets to her side of the clothesline. "You were vague in your letters. Is that question what brought you here?"

"Yes. I hoped you would have some insight for me." All the emotion she'd stifled for months swelled in her throat. Her words came out in a whimper. "But then Justin showed up and now everything is ruined."

John's eyebrows crinkled. "Ruined?"

"Yes." She tried to swallow her emotions—champions didn't cry—but her nose stung and tears blurred her vision. "Now we're looking for ways to survive without sunlight and—"

"God will provide for us."

Once the flood gates opened, her words gushed out. "And Revel is racing across the Land to tell all the overseers to prepare for famine, and we've been searching for the Global guy but can't find him, and even though Connor is certain the guy is dead, Justin says he is only biding his time and will kill us all, and I'm not afraid for myself, but Sophia is terrified and I think Lydia is too. That's probably why Connor is saying the guy is dead—so that Lydia won't freak out, but Justin says he is coming and the freeze is coming and it's on me to protect everyone and—"

John held up a halting hand. "God will protect us. Not you, not Connor."

"But Justin said—"

He squeezed her shoulder. "You have prepared agricultural suggestions for the villages, and it was very much appreciated. Whether there is a two-year winter or not, the Land will be better off because of your work."

Her tears stopped flowing, but her voice had yet to regain its strength. "What about the Global guy? If Connor isn't keeping watch and his security team is disbanded, I'm the only person who can protect us."

He shook his head.

She didn't know what that meant. "Do you agree with Connor that the man is dead, or do you think he is alive but I shouldn't worry about it? If that's it, please don't say it's because I'm a woman."

A warm grin widened his gray beard. "You are not responsible for our protection or for our provision."

"But whenever anything bad happens, I can't just sit around. I have to do something."

"You did. You helped Lydia and Sophia with gray leaf tree research. You completed the research reports we asked you to prepare."

She wiped her cheek on the back of her hand. "But what do I do *now*?"

He pointed at the laundry basket.

A short laugh escaped her tight throat. "Yeah, I will help with the chores while I'm here, but that doesn't occupy me all day. I'll be done with this soon, and what then?"

He sidestepped the laundry baskets on the ground and resumed hanging the wet towels. "Then you can work on committing those verses to memory."

It wasn't what she expected him to say, but she had learned long ago that it was best to do whatever John Colburn suggested. "Yes, sir. Thank you."

While Andrew napped that afternoon and Lydia and Sophia worked out in the medical cottage, Bailey lay on her belly on the guestroom bed and went through John's list of the scriptures she should memorize.

She copied each verse from her Bible onto a small square of gray leaf paper and embellished it with little drawings of the gray leaf tree or flowering vines or whichever plant the verse brought to her botanist mind. It took her most of the afternoon, but she ended up with a deck of scripture cards that could rival any gift set available for sale in America a decade ago.

When voices flowed down the hallway from the kitchen, she closed her Bible and went to help prepare dinner. She wasn't much of a cook, but she enjoyed how the whole family buzzed around the Colburn kitchen at dinner time. Someone always gave her a task, and she loved being made a part of the family.

As she rounded the sofa in the living room, she could see Lydia at the kitchen stove and Sophia walking to the pantry. Andrew was sitting on the floor, banging on a saucepan with a wooden spoon. Connor and John's voices murmured between the rowdy bangs.

Bailey stepped into the kitchen and headed straight for the sink to wash her hands—she knew Lydia's rules—but someone was already there, soaping up. A grin tugged at her lips as she sidled up beside Revel. "I didn't expect you back until the weekend."

He smiled as he rinsed the soapy lather from his strong hands. "I'm sorry: I don't speak American. When exactly does the week end?"

She playfully bumped her hip into his. "Very funny."

While she washed her hands, he dried his with a hand towel Lydia had embroidered with little yellow daisies. He hadn't shaved his face since he'd left, but a week's worth of scruff suited him. His blue cotton shirt with its cuffed sleeves and dusty shoulders suited him. He'd left his boots at the door according to Lydia's house rules, and the hole in one of his wool socks suited him too.

When she released the foot pedal to stop the flow of water from the faucet, he offered her the towel. "How did you get prettier since last time I saw you?"

She snapped the towel out of his hands but didn't hold back her smile. "You say that every time you stop at the inn."

"And it's as true in Good Springs as it is in Falls Creek."

The voices around the room quieted enough to make her acutely aware that everyone else was as curious about their relationship as she was. She held back her response to his compliment and hung the towel on its hook by the sink. "How is everyone at the inn doing?"

He shrugged. "They seemed to be doing well. Zeke is proud of his new front teeth and that he lost more baby teeth."

"Did the tooth fairy leave him anything?"

"The what?"

"Never mind." Despite her silly words, her serious thoughts were locked on the man before her. Her Revel was back, and nothing else mattered.

Wait, *her* Revel?

Before she could analyze the thought, Sophia walked between them and set a colander of potatoes in the sink. Lydia spoke up from the other side of the kitchen. "Rinse those off, Revel, then get to peeling. And Bailey, get to chopping."

"Yes, ma'am," they responded in unison.

While Bailey lounged on her bed that night, she read the scripture cards by the moonlight that filtered through the old-lady lace curtains. One by one, she flipped the cards, reading the verse, then closing her eyes and reciting the words from the image in her mind. As she came to the verse John had quoted today while they did laundry, she paused. *Two are better than one…*

She had missed Revel while he was gone and was happy he was now in the next room over. Whenever he was near, she felt more peace than she had since she first came to faith in Christ.

By morning, the scripture cards were scattered on the bed and a few had fallen to the floor. Though past sunrise, the room was barely light enough to see. She sucked in a breath and rushed to the window in her nightgown.

Dark clouds billowed in from the ocean. They didn't look like ash clouds, but like the normal clouds that blew in from the east before a weather front. And the ash would supposedly come from the west in the upper atmosphere. Surely there was no need to panic.

Then again, the ash could be above those rainclouds and that was why it seemed so dark this morning. Or maybe it had simply been a while since she'd awoken to a cloudy sky and so she'd forgotten how dark the Colburns' guest room was on such a morning.

Either way, she dressed quickly then frequently glanced out the kitchen windows while helping Lydia and John prepare breakfast.

Revel snapped his suspenders over his shoulders as he sauntered into the kitchen. He scanned the bowls waiting on the countertop and carried them to the table. "Morning, all." Though he said *all*, he looked at her while he spoke.

She mumbled the best reply she could—considering it was morning—and finished peeling the hardboiled eggs.

Sophia stepped into the kitchen through the open back door, holding up a pail. "Fresh milk."

John pulled a tray of hot cinnamon rolls out of the oven. "Thank you, Sophia."

Lydia switched a sleepy-eyed Andrew to her other hip, then used her free hand to ladle oatmeal from a stove pot into small porcelain bowls. She glanced at Sophia. "You were very brave to go out to the barn alone this morning. Did you see anything… unusual?"

While Sophia shook her head, Connor shuffled into the room. "Mercer will be down in a few minutes." He went straight for the cupboard where the coffee cups were kept. "Who wants coffee?" While he carried the cups to the table, he looked out the window and then at Revel. "We have to get the hay into the loft before it rains today. I need all hands on deck."

Bailey loved the muscle-burning workout of packing hay in the Colburn's barn loft. "I'll help."

"Great. Thanks, Jeans."

She appreciated how Connor didn't flinch at her doing what the people here considered men's work, but Revel raised an eyebrow at her. She appreciated his old-fashioned chivalry and loved his willingness to let her be herself.

John took Andrew from Lydia and lowered the boy into the highchair. "I will cancel my meeting this morning and help."

Justin lumbered into the room with bedhead hair and sleep marks on his face.

Connor barely flicked a glance at his former co-pilot. He pulled out Lydia's chair for her then said to John,

"Actually, Mercer will help me haul in the hay. If Revel and Bailey can get it packed in the loft, the four of us should be able to knock out the job in a few hours."

Everyone looked at Justin, who wasn't awake enough to know or care what had been assigned to him. He simply rubbed both hands over his face, then reached for his coffee.

John nodded once at Connor. "Very well."

Andrew licked the oatmeal from his spoon. "I help too, Daddy."

Connor rubbed a hand over his son's head. "Not this time, pal. We'll have to work fast. You stay here and help your mama."

Lydia laid a cinnamon roll on Andrew's plate and cut it to bite-sized pieces. "No, I have a house call to make this morning."

Sophia spoke up quickly. "Andrew may stay with me. I'm bottling gray leaf oil in the office this morning, so we will have to stay here in the house."

John laid down his fork. "No, Sophia, you should continue your work. While Lydia makes her house call this morning, I will take Andrew with me to the chapel." He dipped his bearded chin at his grandson. "It is time you learned the profession, Andrew."

While the others chuckled, Bailey glanced across the table at Revel. He wouldn't have a son to teach his profession to if he married her. Thanks to the Unified States offering college grants in exchange for sterilization, she couldn't have children. Not that she wanted kids. Not a baby anyway. She wouldn't know what to do with a baby.

Or maybe it was easier to tell herself she didn't want what she couldn't have.

And it had never mattered to her until now. Perhaps it wouldn't matter to Revel. He'd already bucked the Land's tradition by not accepting his father's inheritance. And he once told her he could see himself taking in an orphan someday. She would certainly like the opportunity to foster an older child—maybe a wayward teen—so she could be for them what Mrs. Polk was for her.

Revel met her gaze and she instantly looked down at her plate, a mixture of guilt and embarrassment warming her cheeks. Why was she even thinking about this? Everything in her used to cringe at the thought of being a wife and mother, and here she was analyzing the prospect.

Something had changed. It shouldn't have. She was still the same person as she was a year ago, just more mature, more settled, more at peace.

So what if she thought about Revel all the time now and how he truly knew her and truly seemed to love her? She was still an independent woman. Just because her feelings for Revel were inexplicably changing didn't mean her life had to change. She had a job and a room at the inn. She had friends who were like family. What more could she possibly want?

The lurking feeling of lack—that unanswerable question that had haunted her for weeks—wasn't even present at the moment.

That would have to suffice as proof she didn't need to complicate her life by trying to entwine it with someone else's.

She gave Revel a silly look that made him smile. Then she turned to Sophia to talk gray leaf research and determined to not think of what John had said about marriage being God's highest earthly blessing for humanity.

John was occupied with telling Andrew about Jesus, while the boy stuffed his little mouth with pieces of cinnamon roll. Lydia was asking Justin how he felt this morning, even though she'd released him from her medical care two days ago. His bruises were gone, and he said the gray leaf medicine had completely healed his broken nose.

Connor scarfed down his food with military speed and left the table. Revel was close behind him while they stacked their plates by the sink. Bailey downed the last of her coffee and followed them to the door.

Connor looked back at the dawdling Justin, who was picking at his food, then he said to Revel and Bailey, "You two can go to the barn and get the loft ready. I'll drag him out there in a few minutes."

As Bailey and Revel walked the worn path of flattened grass across the lawn to the barn, he told her about his evening at the inn and that everyone sent their greetings. As they passed the chicken coop, he had to raise his voice to talk over the unusually loud clucking.

Before they reached the barn doors, a cold wind blew her hair across her forehead. She wished she'd put on her hooded sweatshirt, but once she was working in the hayloft, she would warm up.

As they stepped into the dark barn, she turned back to look at the incoming clouds. Tall puffs swirled high toward the east, blocking the sunrise. She pointed up at the brewing storm. "It's coming from the ocean. Definitely just a normal rainstorm."

Revel paused in the doorway. "You don't think it has anything to do with Mercer's ash clouds?"

"No, but I do think that is what we should name it: Mercer's Ash Clouds."

Even though she grinned, Revel didn't smile. There was something about his seriousness that delighted her, attracted her. He gave the sky one more glance and charged across the barn to the ladder for the hay loft. She waited for him to clear the ladder as she'd been taught, then climbed up too.

He threw open the shuttered loft windows where Connor and Justin would hoist up the hay, then he pulled two pitchforks off the tool rack on the wall and handed her one. "We need to fork the last of this hay down the shoot to the feed bins below before we pack in the new hay."

They worked together in perfect rhythm. While one loaded their pitchfork, the other unloaded, back and forth, alternating movements like a dance. It reminded her of practicing martial arts forms with the other black belts on her team in high school. Except this felt different. Everything she did with Revel felt different, pleasant.

Her shoulder muscles quickly warmed with the work. She wanted to open the window on the east side of the loft so the breeze would blow through, but she didn't want to break their stride. Bits of hay and dust filled the air around her. Most of the guys tied on a handkerchief so they wouldn't breathe in all the dust, but there was no way she could tolerate having something cover her nose and mouth. Just thinking about it sent a wave of claustrophobia that broke her focus. She didn't feel that horrid sensation often since overcoming it to save Tim last year, but some scars never healed completely. She just needed to slow down for a minute and focus on the task at hand.

She dropped the hay from her pitchfork and paused, looking over the loft railing.

Revel stopped too. "You all right?"

"Yeah. Fine." She propped her pitchfork against the railing and walked past him to the other window, hay straw sliding under her boots. "We need to get a breeze flowing up here."

Revel wiped his forehead with his sleeve. "Agreed."

She flipped the metal hook from its clasp and freed the window shutters. The wind blew them open and swirled hay dust through the loft and out the opposite window. The barn air quickly cooled and cleared.

"See?" she said as she walked back to where they were working.

He winked at her. "Much better."

She still didn't like the winking, but it wouldn't stop. As she passed him and reached for her pitchfork, her foot slid on loose straw. Her body immediately braced for a fall the way it had been trained to, but instead of hitting the wooden planks, Revel caught her.

Her instinct was to laugh at herself while Revel steadied her, yet the look in his eyes captured her breath. His hands were still gripping her arms. "Sure you're all right?"

Her answer came out more faintly this time. "Yeah. I'm fine. Don't worry about me."

He slowly released her then brushed his hands together. "I know you don't want my help, Bailey, but whenever you fall, I will catch you."

Though he turned to go back to his work, she didn't move. All at once, the truth hit her: This was what John meant. "Two are better than one."

He halted mid-step and turned back to her. Without a word he locked her gaze and stepped close enough only the breeze blew between them. His hand returned to her arm, gently this time.

She waited for him to say something. Or herself. Anything. Someone had to break the silence. Someone had to laugh or look away.

He only moved closer, his face a whisper from hers.

She hadn't been kissed since ninth grade and that incident was stupid and sloppy. That guy was stupid and sloppy. Afterward, Coach told her not to let another boy distract her, and she'd obeyed for over a decade now.

Revel wasn't a boy, nor was he stupid or sloppy. If he kissed her now, she would let him.

But he didn't.

He simply stood close. So closely she should be freaking out, but she wasn't. She was at perfect peace.

At last he spoke, his gaze fixed on her lips. "They are back with the hay load."

She didn't care about hay or work or outsiders or anything, and wasn't even sure what words came out of her mouth. She only wondered what his whisker stubble would feel like against her skin. "Are you ready?"

"Ready?" A faint grin curved his mouth. "Oh, I've been waiting for this my whole life."

"We aren't talking about stacking the hay, are we?"

He shrugged slightly. "What hay?"

She wanted to smile but dared not move.

A clatter came from the wagon below the loft window, then Connor's voice. "Lower the hoist. Revel? Revel, are you up there?"

Revel looked from Bailey's lips to her eyes. He gave her arm a soft squeeze and slowly pulled away, a hint of satisfaction brightening his smile when finally she exhaled. “Yeah, Connor. We’re ready!”

* * *

It took every ounce of willpower Revel had to step away from Bailey, each footstep backward was more reluctant than the last. But it was the right choice. He’d made the mistake of trying to kiss her once before, and she didn’t want it then. He wasn’t eager to make that mistake again.

His lips tingled with anticipation as he left her standing there by the loft railing. This felt different from the last time he’d almost kissed her. She seemed different this time—like she was waiting for him to make a move, wanting him to.

Man, he hoped he hadn’t just missed his chance.

Connor called from below the loft windows, “Lower the hoist.”

Revel leaned out through the wide opening. “Here it comes.”

While Connor and Mercer attached the hoist to the hay loader, Revel glanced back into the dim loft for Bailey, expecting her to still be twenty feet away, but she was close behind him with her gloves on, ready to pull in the load.

No matter how well he thought he knew her, she surprised him.

While they worked, she matched him move-for-move, packing the hay into the loft. She never mentioned what had happened before Connor and Mercer showed up. That was fine with him. Talking wouldn’t help. If she still wasn’t ready for more than friendship, he didn’t want to ruin things by pushing her.

And if she was thinking what he hoped she was thinking, he would have another chance to kiss her.

At least he prayed he would.

The muscles in his upper back burned by the time Connor and Mercer returned with the last load of hay. They'd all worked as fast as they could to beat the rain, and so far it was holding off. Well, they'd all worked hard except Mercer. From what Revel could tell, it was Connor who did all the loading down there.

Even now, Mercer moved lethargically while they hoisted up the last load. Lazy sluggard. Connor might tolerate his former co-pilot's behavior since they had a history together, but John Colburn wouldn't feed and house a slothful man. And Mercer knew in the Land everyone worked their fair share.

Why did he come back here if he didn't want to live by their ways?

Maybe Bailey was right about the reports of a big freeze being a lie from Global, and maybe Mercer was in on it. He had arrived with the government entity's insignia on his clothing. Come to think of it, no one here behaved as though they trusted the man. Whatever he had come to the Land for, it wasn't to help the people here.

Mercer struggled to secure the hooks on his side of the hoist. Revel glanced at Bailey, and she rolled her eyes. He loved that she was bold enough to emote exactly what she was thinking, at least when it came to the people around them. If only she would clearly show him if her feelings for him had changed.

A deep gasp came from below, and Mercer fell to the ground.

Bailey lunged to the window ledge. "Justin, are you okay?"

Mercer didn't answer.

Revel leaned out to see what was happening, but the hay load blocked his view. Before he could look at Bailey again, she was already halfway down the ladder, rushing to check on Mercer. Revel followed, but at a less concerned pace. Lydia had said the man's wounds were healed and he could work. He was probably just trying to return to the Colburns' divan to sleep away his afternoons.

Revel ambled out of the barn and around to the side where the wagon was. Bailey and Connor were both kneeling over Mercer, who had his hands to his sternum and his face contorted.

Connor motioned Revel closer. "Let's lift him onto the back of the wagon. I'll drive him down to the medical cottage."

Mercer pushed himself away from the ground, and wheezed a cough. "No, don't. I'll be fine. Just got winded, that's all."

Connor put a hand on his shoulder. "You're short of breath and as pale as a ghost. I'm taking you to Lydia."

"Fine, but I can walk there."

Connor and Bailey stayed on either side of Mercer as he rose. As soon as he stood upright, his knees buckled and he melted to the hay-strewn ground, completely unconscious.

Connor lifted his chin at Revel. "Grab his legs. Let's lift him onto the wagon."

CHAPTER TEN

Justin regained consciousness when Connor and Revel laid him on the cot in Lydia's office. The doctor wanted everyone but Sophia out while she examined Justin. Bailey trailed behind the guys as they walked through the rain to the house. She paused to watch the droplets hit her hands. Was this normal rain or was it the prelude to Earth's next ice age?

She could examine the droplets for ash particles if Lydia's microscope was more powerful.

That didn't matter right now. The coming freeze didn't seem important since Justin was in the medical office, drifting in and out of consciousness.

She hadn't felt this nervous when he needed medical attention last week; she'd only been annoyed he was here in the Land. There was no reason for her to be anxious now, yet she bit the nail on her left ring finger until there was nothing to chew. She switched to her pinkie nail while she stood inside the kitchen door and stared out the window at the medical cottage.

Rain poured from the sky in flowing sheets, quickly turning the lawn's low points into puddles. Thunder rumbled in a way that made her wish she were sleeping, but considering something was seriously wrong with Justin, not even a lovely rain shower could relax her.

Connor and Revel sat in silence at the table behind her. The one time she glanced back, Revel was watching her while Connor was staring at the floor. He was probably thinking about all the missions he and Justin had flown together or about their time in training. Who knows what all they'd been through together over the years.

Her eyes moved from the medical cottage's door to its curtained windows and back to the door, hoping at any moment Sophia would come out to tell them the prognosis. Or better yet, she wanted Lydia to come out herself, because that would mean Justin was well enough he didn't need the physician's constant care.

Maybe he had simply overworked himself too soon after his ungraceful arrival on the shore last week. It had taken him longer to respond to the gray leaf medicine and recover from a broken nose that it had for her to recover from the arrow wound last year, but she'd just chalked it up to his being older or tired or less fit. But now he'd blacked out. Maybe something really was wrong with him. Something serious.

Fear rattled her insides. She hated that feeling. She needed to focus. What did Coach always tell her? Okay, first she had to identify her true fear.

That was simple: It was loss. She was afraid of losing Justin. But why? She wasn't particularly fond of him. Still, he was the reason she was in the Land and the reason she'd met her Colburn relatives and the reason she learned Tim was her biological father.

Even so, she and Justin weren't friends. Not really.

Before she could reason out her feelings, the medical cottage door opened. Lydia stepped outside. She shielded her face from the rain with one hand and raised her skirt with the other as she dashed to the house.

When Bailey opened the door for the doctor, Connor stood so abruptly his chair screeched on the kitchen floor. Revel stood too, but much more slowly, smoothing the creases in his pant legs as he stood.

Connor snatched a dish towel from its hook by the sink without taking his eyes off Lydia. He handed it to her. "How is he?"

She dabbed at the raindrops on her neck and arms with the towel. "He is fading in and out of consciousness."

Connor crossed his arms. "Like he did when he first arrived?"

"Worse. Much worse."

Bailey stopped biting her fingernails. She'd expected Lydia to say Justin was fine and they could go visit him, but instead she put on her doctorly air and leveled her chin. "His present condition isn't related to the landing. Justin said he has been experiencing these spells for the past three months.

"While listening to his heart last week, I heard a murmur. He said he knew about it and his doctor in America hadn't been concerned. But when I listened to his heart moments ago, the murmur is much more pronounced."

Connor furrowed his brow. "What type of murmur?"

"It's an aortic arrhythmia, which can be caused by a mitral value problem. My first thought was that it's from a bodily infection, but he says he hadn't been sick or broken a bone, until his facial wounds last week."

Bailey knew athletes who over-trained and ended up with arrhythmias, but she'd never heard of a mitral value problem. The fear in her stomach began to burn. "Is it a birth defect?"

Lydia looked at her the way a teacher looks at a pupil. "That is a possibility."

Connor shook his head. "The navy physicians would not have missed a heart defect when he enlisted. It has to be from something else."

Bailey was less concerned with when and where he developed the condition. "Will the gray leaf medicine cure it?"

Everyone silently waited for Lydia to answer. She kept her voice steady and her hands folded. "That will be our first course of action—gray leaf tea and plenty of rest. If his condition was caused by anything bacterial or viral, the gray leaf will cure it. If not, all that's left is mechanical."

Bailey swallowed the air in her mouth. "Meaning he will die from this since you can't do open-heart surgery here."

Lydia gave her forearm a gentle squeeze. "I'm sorry, Bailey. I wish I could do more for him. I will prepare the gray leaf tea immediately." She gave Connor a look that meant something only a spouse would know. Then she looked at Bailey, her voice softer. "Justin asked if you would visit him while I prepare his medicine."

Connor put his hand on Bailey's back. "Do you need me to come with you?"

Why they acted like Bailey had a puppy dying, she didn't know. Connor had known Justin longer than she had. If anyone needed support, it should be him. She shrugged off his hand. "No, it's fine. I'm fine. He probably just wants to whine about not having a phone or television in the Land or something stupid." She glanced at Revel. "I'll be back in a minute."

Even as she spoke the words, she knew she wouldn't return for a long while.

Sophia was removing Justin's shoes and socks when Bailey walked into the medical office. He was lying flat on his back on the cot across the room. His eyes were closed, so Bailey looked to Sophia for a signal of what she should do.

Sophia opened her hand to a ladder-back chair near the head of the cot and whispered, "You may sit there."

The skin around Justin's eyes was darker than it had been an hour ago. It wasn't bruising from his accident; that was all gone. The shadows made him look like he was in his late fifties instead of his early thirties. As she sat, he drew a deep breath and opened his eyes a sliver. "Bailey?"

"I'm here."

"Hey, beautiful."

She ignored that. "Lydia is making you some gray leaf tea."

He lifted his head a few inches off the pillow and crinkled his brow at Sophia. "Make yourself scarce for a few minutes, sweetie."

Bailey nudged his shoulder. "Be nice to her."

An easy grin creased his freshly shaven cheeks. "That was me being nice."

"Even when you're dying, you're a real piece of work."

"Who says I'm dying?"

She simply stared at him. Bedside manners had never been her specialty.

Once Sophia closed the door to her room upstairs, Justin laid his head back down. "All right, fine. I'm dying. That's why I came to the Land."

The annoyance she'd felt last week returned in a wave that flushed all fear and pity from her system. She stood and hovered over him. "So that whole story about a volcanic ash cloud and a two-year winter was a lie?"

He lifted a weak hand. "No, that's all true."

"But you didn't come here to warn us about that. You came for gray leaf medicine because you knew something was wrong with your heart, didn't you?"

"You're a sharp girl."

A sharp girl who would've kicked him if he wasn't already down. "Why not just have the Global doctors do heart surgery on you?"

"There are no Global doctors. Not unless you're part of the elite."

"Which you aren't."

He tapped his chest. "Bailey, I know it's bad—whatever is wrong inside me—and gray leaf medicine is my only hope. You were right when you said it took me months to get assigned to a ship in the South Atlantic and then manipulate it to be near the Land's coordinates on the equinox. And I had no way of knowing when the nuclear war would start or that a bunch of volcanos would spew ash into the upper atmosphere." He covered his heart. "But I'm glad it happened when it did because I was able warn you and hopefully save the Land… while the Land saves me."

"That's what you think the gray leaf will do? Save you?" She plopped down on the stiff wooden chair. "Justin, you had two doses of gray leaf tea last week, and you still have this mitral valve problem or whatever it is.

And Lydia says it's rapidly getting worse. Do you really think another dose of gray leaf will repair something so serious?"

"Maybe. I don't know." A look shaded his face and wiped all arrogance from his eyes. It was a look she'd never seen on him before. Defeat. "No, probably not."

She remembered feeling that way when she had to destroy his gray leaf saplings back in Virginia. Tim had encouraged her then to try to find the Land. It had taken all of her courage to leave the Unified States during a world war and seek out the hidden island Justin told her about. She had wondered if he was lying then, and it turned out to be true.

The Land had been her only hope for life once, and now it was Justin's only hope too. She bolstered her voice to share some of her courage with him. "Yeah well, let's give it a shot. There is always a chance. The wonderful Doctor Bradshaw says your condition might be from an infection or something. If it is, the gray leaf could cure it."

Lydia stepped into the office with a tea tray, looking more like it was time for a social sip rather than time for life-giving medicine that knocked most adults unconscious for hours.

Justin sat up to accept the tea from Lydia. He raised the dainty porcelain cup as if toasting a celebration. "Here's to last chances."

He swallowed the tea in a few short gulps, then reclined on the cot and reached for Bailey's hand. "Stay with me until I'm out, okay?"

His simple words pierced her heart. She'd heard them before when her roommate was dying during the water poisoning, and when Coach died of the plague, and when Tim drank the gray leaf medicine last year at the inn.

Now Justin was holding the same hand they had all held.

"Okay." Even as she mumbled her agreement, she squeezed his hand and let it go. She would stay until he was out, but not while he died, if he died.

She couldn't go through that again. Ever.

Since he usually irritated her, tested her, and tried to tempt her, she hadn't thought he meant much to her. But he meant something to her. He was the reason she was here. She didn't want him in her life or in the Land, but she didn't want him to die either.

And she didn't want to lose another person.

This was why she couldn't let herself fall in love with Revel. If it hurt this much to lose an acquaintance—a really annoying acquaintance—how much more would it hurt to lose a husband? She already loved Revel more than she'd promised herself she ever would, and that love was growing.

She shouldn't let it. It would only end in loss. Love always led to loss.

Justin's head softly lulled to the side.

Lydia stepped to the cot. She checked his pulse, then covered his legs with a blue wool blanket. "He will sleep for the rest of the day, probably through the night too."

Bailey stood and backed away from the cot, unable to speak. She stepped outside and closed the cottage door behind her. Rain pelted her face. Instead of running to the house, she leaned against the cottage door and let the water hit her skin. She couldn't face another death.

"Bailey?" the voice she longed to hear called out to her. "Bailey?"

She opened her eyes to see Revel standing in the kitchen doorway, his eyes full of concern.

Everything in her told her to run the other way, to not let him close to her—not to her physically and especially not to her emotionally. But that seemed cowardly. That type of running didn't require strength. Hiding didn't require courage.

Her heart filled with peace when she looked at him, truly looked at him. In his eyes she saw whatever it was that she'd been missing in life. Whenever she was near him, she didn't feel that miserable longing. But letting him near meant the possibility of one day losing him too.

In all the martial arts matches she'd fought, in all the trails she'd faced in life, she'd never needed more courage than she did now.

Maybe it took more courage to love than to fight.

With a silent prayer for wisdom and strength, she peeled herself away from the cottage and jogged to the kitchen door, sopping wet.

Revel pulled her into a warm hug and kissed the top of her head. "Are you all right?"

"No." She laid her head against his chest. "But I will be." Instant peace wrapped her tighter than his arms.

She had to stay in control of her feelings now more than ever. If she was wrong about Revel—about their relationship—she wouldn't ruin their friendship.

No, she wouldn't stop her growing love for Revel or whatever this was happening in her heart, but she certainly wouldn't tell him how she felt until she was certain.

* * *

Revel carried his bags out of the Colburns' guest room before dawn the next morning. The rain had continued through the night at a light but steady pace, ensuring a miserable journey today. The sky would be too dark to read the hours and the roads would be too soggy to coax Blaze into a decent trot.

He didn't want to leave now, in the rain, with all that was going on here.

Mostly, he didn't want to leave Bailey.

With no light in the vacant parlor, he couldn't read the clock on the wall behind John's armchair. The faint glow of a lantern streamed out of the kitchen. He expected to see John sitting at the table drinking coffee and preparing for this morning's sermon, but it was Bailey.

She glanced up from the papers she was writing on. "Oh hey, Rev."

"Good morning." He looked over her shoulder as he passed the table to put his bags by the back door. "What are you writing?"

She capped a silver pen, then stretched her neck to both sides. "I just finished the last copy of my recommendation report. You needed three copies for the northern villages, right?"

"That's right." He circled back to the table and pulled a chair out to sit beside her. "I thought you were planning to finish that last night."

"I was, but I went out to the cottage to sit with Justin instead."

Revel's chest hardened. "Did he awaken?"

"Not yet." She tapped the papers on the table to square their edges then offered them to him. "But he will soon. I'm sure of it. I know he can beat this thing. He'll be back to his nauseatingly arrogant self in no time."

A glimmer of hope relaxed him, but it wasn't hope for Mercer's recovery. It was a wicked hope—a desire to be rid of the man who constantly called Bailey *beautiful* and leered at her when she wasn't aware. He took the papers from her hand. "How long did you stay out there with him?"

"Most of the night." She yawned. "I just meant to go check on him, but Sophia was tired, so I told her to go up to bed and I stayed with him."

"Why?"

Bailey wrinkled her nose at him. "Because he.. because I… I don't know. I care about him; that's *why*."

A surge quickened his pulse. He wanted to stamp his fist on the table and demand she tell him the nature of her relationship with Mercer, but suddenly he realized he was sitting in John's chair at the head of the table. John Colburn would never behave in such a manner.

Revel took extra care to hold his tongue as he slowly stood, folded the papers, and carried them to his satchel.

When he bent down to secure Bailey's neatly copied pages in his bag, she continued talking. "Yesterday when he asked me to stay with him, he talked like he would die soon. I swore to myself I wouldn't watch another person die, so I left as soon as he was under the gray leaf medicine."

Her care for Mercer was trying Revel's last strand of patience. He managed to speak despite his clamped teeth. "So why did you go back to him last night?"

Her voice lightened with every word. "I thought about how it must feel. I know if it were me, I wouldn't want to be alone. Besides, if it wasn't for Justin, I wouldn't be here in the Land. Also, I went back to sit with him because if something feels like it is too hard for me to face, I know I have to do it. I have to prove to myself that I am strong enough."

"So are you?"

"Am I what?"

He walked back to the table and stood with both hands planted on its surface. More venom slipped into his voice than he intended. "Are you strong enough to watch Mercer die?"

"Revel!" She looked like she'd just swallowed a bug. "What is wrong with you this morning?"

The more angry she became, the better he felt. He had spent years with everyone disappointed in him. Perhaps that was his lot in life. He wasn't destined to have a loving wife like every other man he knew. He was destined to be alone, riding from village to village, with those he cared about angry with him.

Even as he spoke he disgusted himself more than he could possibly repulse her. "Maybe you went to him because you missed him. Maybe the reason his arrogance aggravates you so much is that you're fond of him. Maybe the reason you didn't want to watch him die is that you're in love with him."

She pushed her chair under the table and calmly gathered her things without looking at him. "Nope. You're wrong."

"Am I?"

"Yes, you are so very wrong. You're jealous of a dying guy, you're acting like a jerk, and you're not being a very good friend right now. But all that I can forgive because…" Finally she looked him in the eye, and where he expected to see violence, he only saw a tired smile that did little to cover her deep sadness. "Because… I thought you understood me."

He remembered their conversation by the fire when they were traveling to Good Springs. She'd said she would rather be understood than loved. He'd thought he could give her both, yet at the moment he was giving her neither. He peeled his hands from the table, and his anger melted into regret.

Regret he understood.

Regret was an old friend who never let him down.

He picked up his bags and crossed their straps over his shoulders. "Tell John I had to leave early because of the rain."

"Don't you want breakfast before you go?"

"No."

"How long will you be gone?"

"At least a week. Maybe two."

A crack in her voice dropped her volume. "The Fosters' barn party is next Tuesday. Will you be back in time?"

"Probably not."

Her mouth fell open slightly, and her hands hung limply at her sides. "Oh."

Everything in him wanted to say he would be back and he would take her to the Fosters' party and they would dance all night, but she wasn't his to take. Nor should she be. She deserved a better man.

He reached for the door knob. "Enjoy the party. I'm sure you will find plenty of dancing partners. Perhaps Mr. Mercer will be fully recovered by then."

CHAPTER ELEVEN

After Revel left Good Springs, the hours passed like months for Bailey. She didn't return to the medical cottage to check on Justin for the rest of the morning—not because Revel had made an issue of it, but because she had to get herself dressed for church while half asleep.

She almost nodded off during John's church sermon, and she wanted to curl up in the back of the covered wagon on the rainy ride home from the chapel. She would've slept right where she was, but Andrew was having fun giving bits of hay to each passenger. First he handed one through the canvas opening to his dad on the front bench, then he gave one to Sophia, who sat opposite Bailey in the covered back, and then to Bailey. When his hands were empty, the little boy picked more straw out of the bales used for seating and handed them out in the same order again and again.

Lydia had stayed behind with Justin while the rest of the household went to church. She'd insisted John go to the Fosters' for their weekly after-church luncheon, but he insisted on coming home because of Justin's condition. Watching Lydia and John together always made Bailey miss her father. She'd only known Tim as her father for a few days before his death, but he'd truly been a father to her for years—a good father, just like John Colburn.

As they turned onto the property, Bailey peered out the wagon cover's back opening, wishing Revel were riding behind them the way he had ridden behind the McIntoshes when he escorted them to Good Springs.

He did that a lot on his courier route—escorted families who were afraid to travel alone. He also helped traders who'd overloaded their wagons or had broken down along the road. He was always helping someone somewhere. Even now he was delivering the warning to the northern villages that there might be an extra-long winter coming to the Land.

She thought back to their argument before he left. There was no reason for him to be jealous of Justin; she didn't love the outsider beyond her love for any human being. However, the fact that Revel was jealous of her being alone with Justin meant he thought of her as his.

His. What a weird concept.

She was a person, not property.

That was one aspect of marriage that made her cringe. She didn't want to belong to anyone—to anyone except the Lord.

And to a family. She'd always longed to be part of a family. And now she knew her Colburn relatives in the Land and was beginning to feel like she belonged to them. But belonging to a man seemed… antiquated.

Then again, there was something flattering about his flare of jealousy. She felt like a ditzy school girl to even admit it to herself. Still, it was true.

So maybe she did want to belong with Revel. Not belong *to* him, but with him.

There was a difference. It might not mean much to the people here, but it meant a lot to her. The difference meant her being able to make a lifetime commitment or not.

It was a difference of considering herself in a partnership versus being property.

One concept she could consider; the other she couldn't tolerate.

Sometimes in the Land it was hard to know which archaic rules she would be held to if she ever got married. The way Solo or Isaac or Levi treated his wife differed greatly from the way Naomi's parents or Sophia's parents had behaved. That was probably true in every era and every place.

But she didn't have to consider the manner in which each man in the Land treated women. She only had to consider Revel's manner.

In fact, she wouldn't consider entering into a committed relationship with anyone but Revel.

As John pulled the wagon to a stop, Bailey determined to forget Revel's rude behavior this morning and not let it ruin the rest of her day or their relationship. He meant too much to her for such trivialities.

She released the handful of hay straw Andrew had gifted her and gave him a quick tickle. His bubbly laughter smothered the sound of the raindrops tapping on the canvas wagon cover.

Connor lifted Andrew out of the back of the wagon, then John offered a hand to Sophia as she climbed down. Once she was clear of the gate, he offered his hand to Bailey.

"No, thanks." She lifted the hem of her blue church dress and climbed down by herself.

Lydia was in the kitchen and had already scooped Andrew up in a motherly welcome when Bailey stepped into the warm house.

Connor gave his wife an almost-too-long kiss. “How is Mercer?”

The doctor wiped her lips and shifted her son to the other hip. “He’s still sleeping. No change in his heart yet.”

Connor showed neither worry nor hope. He simply shucked off his wet jacket and hung it by the door, chatting casually as if they were discussing the weather. “It’s only been a day. He slept longer than that when he drank gray leaf tea last week.”

Lydia lowered Andrew to the floor. After the boy ran to the living room to play, Lydia’s voice took on a professional tone. “Yes, but during his treatment last week he awoke several times and drank water, then went back to sleep.”

The room went still. Lydia looked at Connor then John, and finally her gaze settled on Bailey. “Mr. Mercer hasn’t stirred in over twenty-four hours. He’s showing signs of dehydration.”

Bailey’s empty stomach knotted. “Can’t you figure out how to give him an IV or whatever?”

Connor narrowed his eyes at Bailey, warning her to watch her tone. “Not in the Land.”

John put his kind hand on Bailey’s shoulder but looked at his daughter. “Thank you, Lydia. We know you are doing all you can for Mr. Mercer. We will continue to pray for him.”

Bailey ignored her hungry stomach and barely touched her lunch. The rain didn’t stop all afternoon. Each drop tinked on her window like a hollow sneer. The man she most cared about was riding across the Land in this miserable weather, and the man she was most concerned about was next door, dying.

She sat by the window in her borrowed bedroom and prayed for them both, but felt no better. John always said her ability to trust in the Lord would be directly influenced by how much she meditated on God's Word. She opened the bedside table's top drawer and withdrew the stack of scripture cards she'd made. While reading them, she allowed the truth of each verse to linger in her mind.

After dinner, the rain stopped but the clouds were still thick, blocking all hope of a much needed sunset. Lydia didn't return to the house for dinner, so Bailey took her a plate. It was the only way she could force herself to go to the medical cottage.

Justin hadn't moved since she last saw him. His skin was sallow, his cheeks pitted.

No matter how much she wanted to deny the facts, she touched his hand to say goodbye and left him there on the cot under the woolen blanket and Lydia's expert care.

Sleep smothered Bailey's exhausted mind that night. When bright sunrays slipped through the lacy bedroom curtains the next morning, she sat up in bed with a full surge of hope. She leapt to the window to check the sky. The horizon was blocked by the trees and shrubs in the Colburns' back yard, but everything above that looked clear.

Maybe God had answered her prayer—the whole village's prayer—that the ash layer would pass over the Land somehow.

Her heart filled with more excitement than she'd felt since she almost kissed Revel in the barn loft two days ago. Maybe God had answered their other prayer too. Maybe Justin was awake and healed. Perhaps she'd said goodbye to him too soon.

She tugged on her jeans and her Eastern Shore University sweatshirt, then hurried out of the guestroom for the medical office. Her happy feet came to a quick halt as soon as she stepped into the kitchen.

The back door was wide open, filling the room with chilly morning air. Connor was sitting at the table with his head in his hands, Lydia leaning down to hold him with her head pressed sweetly to his shoulder. Sniffing came from one or both of them. Bailey couldn't tell.

Lydia looked up at her, wiped her eyes, and stood erect. "I'm so sorry, Bailey."

There were those words again. She'd heard them many times over the years and had hoped to never hear them again.

That hope hadn't been realistic. As long as she survived in this fallen world, she would out live someone she cared about.

She lowered herself into the chair opposite Connor, who still hadn't looked up. She didn't want him to. If he was crying, she would lose it.

With the kitchen entrance open, she could hear the medical office door open and close across the path. A moment later, John walked into the kitchen with his shoulders slumped. He didn't speak as he stepped toward the table and gazed at Bailey, his piercing blue eyes encircled with red. She stood and melted in his arms, silently weeping not only for this loss but for all those she'd lost before too.

* * *

Justin hadn't been a member of the Good Springs community before his death, yet most of the villagers attended his burial. As they stood shoulder-to-shoulder in the graveyard, John leaned down to Bailey's ear. "They are all here for Connor, and for you."

After Connor addressed the crowd by saying a few gracious words about Justin's academic and military accomplishments, the villagers whispered their condolences then dispersed.

During the days that followed, Bailey found solace in the quiet hours spent in the Colburn house. Mourning in this room for Justin felt very different from when she'd mourned during Tim's disappearance. There was no deep sadness in her heart now, which in itself made her pensive. Perhaps it was natural to feel less pain since she wasn't truly close to Justin. Grief was like fire: the closer one was to the departed, the more it burned.

Between helping with chores, committing the scripture cards to memory, and fireside evenings in the living room with John, Bailey's thoughts soon returned to the present and her mood lightened. Considering all that had happened—and might still happen—the quiet, simple joy in her heart seemed inexplicable. By God's grace, she had survived another loss.

And could enjoy her remaining time at the Colburns'.

One cozy afternoon, she finished her chores then settled on the sofa to read. Her mind stilled as she watched the sunlight move the window blinds' shadow slowly across the book she held. She re-read a sentence for the third time and still couldn't picture the dance steps it described.

John shuffled through the living room on his way to the kitchen. "What are you reading?"

She checked the book's title page. "*Pleasantries and Customs by Abigail Owens written in The Year of Our Lord Nineteen Hundred and Naught.*"

"I see. Did you find it at the library?"

She pointed at the glass-front bookcase across the living room. "Nope. It's yours."

He pursed his lips. "I do not recall owning that title."

"I'm not surprised. It's pretty dull."

That got a quick chuckle out of him. "Have you learned anything from it?"

"Not really. I thought the chapter entitled *Social Dances for Couples and Groups* would give me a hint on what to do at the Fosters' barn party."

"Oh good, so you plan to attend the harvest celebration."

"Of course. This says all members of each household in the village must arrive together at any social function. All attendees must dance at least once to show a congenial spirit." She lowered the boring book to her lap. "I was hoping Revel would be back in time to go so I didn't have to dance with someone who either mashed my toes or was such a Fred Astaire I couldn't keep up. But since he won't back in time," she clapped the book shut, "I guess I'll hope for the toe masher."

John took the book from her, slipped it onto a side table, and offered his hand. "I am not acquainted with Fred Astaire, but I will stay off your toes. Which dance would you like to learn?"

She popped up from the sofa and accepted his hand. "The diagrams in that book weren't very good, but the Waltz looked simplest. Is it?"

"The Waltz will be easiest for you to learn, as it is a simple box step. You must learn to follow the man's direction though, so that might make it difficult for you in spirit."

"Truth." She laughed. "I'll do my best."

"I know you will."

John hummed a tune while he taught her the steps on the well-worn rug in the living room. While the dance was simple enough, when voices flowed from the open back door, she wanted the lesson to end before anyone saw her.

John didn't care if they received an audience. As he turned her slowly through the steps, the stone fireplace passed in front of her vision, then the wall with the clock, then the front door that no one used. When she turned once more, Lydia stood in the kitchen entryway holding a laundry basket on her hip.

John kept dancing but stopped humming. "Hello, Lydia. Would you like the next dance?"

She smiled. "Maybe later, Father."

"Very well." He hummed the final bar, ended the dance, and politely applauded Bailey. It was the first time she'd felt like she was enjoying her time in Good Springs the way she'd imagined she would when she planned this visit.

Lydia set the basket of folded laundry by the staircase. "Did either of you take anything off the clothesline today?"

They both shook their heads.

"Several items are missing." Lydia cocked her head. "It's the oddest thing. Mostly Connor's clothes, and a couple of towels too."

Sophia stepped in from the kitchen, eating an apple. "The coop was completely empty of eggs again this morning."

John scratched his trimmed gray beard. "I noticed a shirt went missing from the line a few days ago. I assumed someone started to take down the laundry and got distracted by another chore."

Lydia's hand flattened against her stomach. "Do you think it is the man who came to the Land with Mr. Mercer?"

Sophia sucked in a breath and covered her gaping mouth.

John patted the air. "Now ladies, Connor saw clear indications that the man was injured and tried to return to the wreckage as the tide came in. The men searched several times and found no sign of him."

Bailey wiped a drip of sweat from her brow. Whether it had formed while she concentrated on the dance steps or from the mention of the Global guy being around the property, she didn't know. After going several days with no sign of him, she had almost believed Connor was right and Koslov was dead. The last thing she wanted to do was send Lydia and Sophia back into constant fear.

John didn't look worried. Lydia grimaced but managed to pick up her laundry basket and relax her face. But Sophia stood frozen in the doorway with a half-eaten apple in her trembling hand.

Bailey tugged on Sophia's sleeve. "Finish your snack and come with me to the vegetable garden. I want to help plant your late crop before I have to go back to Falls Creek."

Sophia snapped out of her fog and looked at Bailey. "Right, very good. Thank you."

While Bailey escorted Sophia out of the parlor, she glanced back at John and Lydia, who had their gazes locked on each other as if they would speak intently once alone.

Connor had to be in denial about Koslov being a threat because he wanted to prove he could live by the Land's pacifist ways. He'd instructed the security team to focus on their work at home and in the fields. And Revel was long gone.

So Mercer had been right: Bailey was the only person who would protect them from Koslov. It was all on her.

CHAPTER TWELVE

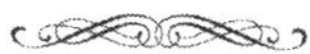

Revel made it to the outskirts of Good Springs just before sundown. There wasn't time to ride to the Colburns', take a shower, and then walk back out here before the barn party, so he stopped at Levi's house on the grassy incline across the road from the Foster farm.

Levi, Mandy, and baby William were preparing to leave, but they let Revel go inside to freshen up for the party. After a quick shower, he wiped the steam from the bathroom mirror and shaved. His body was tired from riding hard all day from the riverboat, but there was no way he was missing the festivities tonight, especially after the way he'd left things with Bailey ten days ago.

Ten long, depressing days ago.

He didn't want to think about the uncomfortable journey in the rain on the way to the northern villages, nor the long wait in each town as its overseer sent word to the village elders to come in from harvesting for an unscheduled meeting. Blaze had needed the restful breaks in every village, but Revel hadn't. He'd planned to be back in Good Springs with Bailey by now.

He buttoned his black waistcoat, tied his new silk cravat under his collar, and left Levi's empty house grateful for friends who understood.

A full oval moon cast its blueish light across Levi's yard, spilling the gray leaf trees' shadows onto the road. Revel crossed it to hike through the crunchy autumn grass to the Fosters' property.

The evening's cool air felt good on his skin after the hot shower. He smoothed his collar and checked his cuffs as he neared the line of wooden tables where the villagers would have eaten dinner together at sunset.

The first time he attended one of the Fosters' annual harvest parties, he'd been young and had worked all summer for Mr. Samuel Foster. Sometimes, he still expected to see the gentle, older man here, but Mr. Foster was in Heaven and this was Everett's farm now.

Music drifted from the massive barn's open doors. Most of the guests were inside, dancing in their finest apparel, boots stomping to the beat. Some were still mingling at the tables outside, mostly the elderly folks who were chatting about the fine weather or the abundant food or their varying health. The light from myriad lanterns streamed out of the barn, illuminating their lined faces, making Revel wish to slowly grow old with Bailey.

Everett stood outside the barn's entrance, shoulders proudly squared, his pretty wife on his arm. They were greeting another late-coming guest.

Good, at least Revel wasn't the only one.

While he waited his turn to speak to the hosts, Mrs. Roseanna Foster lumbered past him carrying a pan of some sweet-smelling dessert. "Hello there, Revel." Mrs. Foster lifted her double chin at a table covered in near-empty serving pans and platters. "We still have roast and beans, but this is the last cobbler to come out of the oven. We would've had more, but a whole pan of my finest cobbler went missing from the stoop while it cooled this afternoon. You better come and get this before it's gone too, dear. Wouldn't want you to miss out!"

"Thank you, Mrs. Foster."

The jovial, middle-aged woman gave him a wink and set her cobbler pan on the picnic table that was being used as a buffet.

Inside the barn, a drum beat counted off the next dance—a folk tune Revel's mother used to have Sybil play on the piano when she wanted the family to dance. The song made him miss his mother. He hadn't been able to visit her when he was in Southpoint because of his rushed journey. Maybe next time.

The other guest walked away from Everett and Bethany, so Revel stepped forward to say hello.

Everett flipped his dark hair off his forehead and spoke with a full voice and relaxed words, sounding more like Connor than a man from Good Springs. "Revel, bro! Welcome."

"Thank you." He shook Everett's hand then gave Bethany a polite kiss on the cheek. "Everything looks lovely tonight."

She beamed. "Thank you. Roseanna did most of the planning and cooking, but she let me help." Her cheeks dimpled when she smiled, making him miss Sybil. "I believe most of the village joined us tonight. We barely had enough dessert."

"So I heard." He glanced across the lantern-lit tables at where Mrs. Foster was nestling a serving spoon into the cobbler. Had she said a whole pan of cobbler went missing today? Was that how Koslov was sustaining himself now—stealing desserts from ladies' porches?

He forced his attention back to Everett. "Was all well in Good Springs while I was away?"

Everett looked past Revel at someone who was approaching them from the barn. He lowered his voice. "I think he wants to fill you in himself."

"Fill me in?" He turned around to see Connor walking toward him.

Connor wore his Sunday jacket and a black neck tie, making him look more like John Colburn than like the warrior who had trained the men here how to fight. "Hey, man. Levi said you were back. Stopped at his place instead of riding into the village for a shower and a shave?"

Revel rubbed his smooth cheek. "That and to let Blaze rest for the night."

The upbeat song ended in the barn. It was followed by laughter and applause, then several couples came out of the barn fanning their sweaty faces.

Connor patted Revel's shoulder. "Let's talk," he said as he led him away from the tables where villagers were starting to gather.

The tone of Connor's voice made Revel's spine stiffen. This was about either Koslov or Mercer, or perhaps the ash cloud had been spotted. He checked the star-spotted sky above. It still seemed clear.

Connor stopped walking when they reached the edge of the barn. "Did you hear Mercer died?"

Instead of feeling relief or triumph, he only thought of Bailey. "No. When?"

"A week ago yesterday."

"I'm sorry. Bailey thought the gray leaf would heal him." He glanced back to make sure no one was near. "Any sign of Koslov?"

Connor shook his head. “The girls keep saying things are going missing outside, but I know Koslov didn’t survive. It has to be someone else.”

“Another outsider?”

Connor shook his head once.

Revel wanted to tell him everything—to come clean both for his conscience and to protect the village, but it was too late now. He’d kept the secret for too long.

Then again, Connor was too smart to be ignoring all the signs that the outsider was still lurking around the village.

Maybe Connor knew Revel had fed Koslov and was testing his loyalty.

After spending his adult life on the road, Revel’s first loyalty was to himself, no matter how much he wanted to change. He met Connor’s gaze. “I’m sorry about Mercer. I know you were acquainted with him for some time.”

Connor pulled at his collar and looked away. “Yeah, well, it’s all a part of the war out there. I have lost a lot of friends over the years.”

“So has Bailey.” The violin began playing a waltz, and Revel looked through the open barn doors, searching for the woman he loved. “How did she take his death?”

When Connor didn’t answer, Revel stopped scanning the crowd for Bailey and looked at Connor, who raised his thick eyebrows. “Ah. I see.”

“You see what?”

“I see why you were in such a hurry to get here tonight.”

Last year, Connor had warned him to not pursue Bailey. He’d said she wasn’t ready for courtship. And he had been right.

Revel waited for Connor to tell him to forget about ever courting her, to set his feelings aside, and to focus on his work. Instead, Connor simply sank his hands into his trouser pockets and took a half step back. "She's in the barn, dancing with John."

Revel craned his neck to look. "Bailey is dancing?"

"They just waltzed past the stage. Go see for yourself."

Revel straightened his cravat and brushed imaginary lint from his sleeves as he walked toward the light that spilled out of the barn along with slow, sweet music.

Most of the crowd danced the waltz while Mandy stood on the platform on the other side of the cavernous room, playing her violin. The new-wood instrument filled the barn with the robust sound only the gray leaf could. He scanned the dancers as they bobbed up and down in the three-four time of the age-old beat.

At last, he caught a glimpse of John Colburn across the room. Connor had said John was dancing with Bailey, but through the ocean of raised heads and hands, Revel couldn't see her face. The slow circular motion of the crowd shifted them closer to him at such a slow pace he left the entrance and followed the perimeter of the dance floor to see if it was indeed Bailey.

John spotted him and gave him a knowing look.

The music slowed with the song's final notes, and the motion of the room collectively wobbled to a halt like an overworked mule.

Bailey saw him then. Every emotion he felt for her seemed to be reflected in her amber eyes. The dancers clapped for Mandy and for each other, but Bailey didn't join the applause until it was already dying down.

John gave Revel's back an encouraging pat, saying nothing and not needing to.

Revel kept his gaze fixed on Bailey. There was nothing else in the world worth looking at.

She wore her blue Sunday dress, had a silver flower-shaped comb pinning half her hair off her face, and a black lace choker encircled her neck. Though her attire was suspiciously the work of Lydia or Sophia, the passionate independence in her defiant eyes was completely her own.

He stepped close enough to hear her breathe. "May I have the next dance?"

"You may." Her whispered reply jolted his heart.

Several musicians joined Mandy and started playing a slow, intricate song.

Bailey pointed at the band without looking away from him. "Is this another waltz?"

He shook his head and took her hand.

"But that's the only dance John taught me."

A soft melody flowed through the room, as gentle as a morning mist that settled over the roads throughout the Land. He breathed in her florally feminine scent and tried to stay focused. "This is what we call a *free dance.* Couples are at liberty to dance however they feel inclined or to not dance at all."

She broke his gaze and looked around at the other couples. "Um…"

He didn't let go of her hesitant fingertips. "Just follow me. You'll be fine."

"Okay." She smiled at him for the first time in ten days. "Sure. Why not?"

He slid one hand around her waist, his fingers melting into her dress's warm fabric. With the other hand he lifted hers, unable to remember any other women he'd ever danced with in his life.

He led Bailey in the casual shuffling steps every man in the Land knew and every woman graciously pretended took talent. The dance floor was filled with other couples doing the same move. That didn't matter; none of it did. Bailey was the only woman in the world and this was the only moment that mattered.

Her hand was soft and small in his, but he knew its true strength and lethal skill. Yet she was allowing him to guide their movement. He leaned down to her ear. "You're letting me lead. Thank you."

She looked up at him, her eyes seeming to offer what he'd asked for once and been denied.

Dare he ask again?

No. Not now.

He didn't really know what she wanted. And if she was thinking what he hoped she was thinking, what came next?

Loving Bailey was like trying to keep a flame for a pet.

If he never got to have her close again, he had her in his arms now. And for once in his life he wouldn't ruin the moment. "You are beautiful."

She glanced down at her dress and blushed slightly, then quickly shielded herself with a humorous eye-roll. Just the fact that she needed to hide her true feelings meant there was something there for him to explore.

* * *

Bailey tried to shrug off Revel's compliment the way she always did, but her soul soaked in his adoration this time and wouldn't let it go. "The girls dolled me up, so I would… well, you know."

"No, I don't know."

His straight-shooting reply chipped away at her armor. "So I'd look beautiful tonight or whatever."

"I didn't say you look beautiful; I said you *are* beautiful, Bailey."

She wanted to freeze time and savor the girly feeling of being slow danced to lovely music by a man who knew her better than anyone else and still liked her. More than liked—he seemed to love her in a way she'd never been loved.

His confident hands guided her effortlessly in the dance. She didn't have to think about her steps. It gave her time to absorb the moment. Things could quickly change in the Land. She wouldn't be able to bask in simple emotions for long.

Neither could she resist them anymore.

The music repeated the last line of its melody, then again. During its third repeat, the tempo slowed, as did Revel's steps. He gazed down at her even while the other couples left the dance floor. His voice was barely audible over the crowd. "I'm sorry for what I said before I left—"

"It's all right."

"No, it wasn't all right. It was wrong and immature and I've regretted it every moment since."

His hair was still damp and marked with comb lines, and he smelled like fresh soap. He must have only been back in town long enough to get dressed, because he hadn't made it to the Colburns' house before she left with John and the others.

"Did you hurry here tonight so you could apologize to me?"

His serious expression softened. “No. I hurried because I missed you, but I’m sure you already knew that.”

She’d hoped, certainly, but hadn’t known for sure. “I missed you too.”

He kept her fingertips in his hand and led her out of the barn. “Come with me.”

As soon as the cool evening air hit her skin, she drew in a long inhale. “I didn’t realize how warm it was in there.”

He glanced back but kept a steady pace while walking her away from the party. “Yeah, barn dances are like gray leaf medicine: they will cure what ails you, but are only good in small doses.”

She loved the way he spoke, his voice, his manners, all of it. Some murmur of agreement escaped her lips, but she wasn’t thinking about herself for once and it felt wonderful.

A chilly breeze blew over the pastures, bringing with it the scents of nature at night. The starry sky hung over them like a bejeweled curtain, and a dozen crickets slowly pulsed with the music of an autumn evening.

He turned at the end of the barn and stopped when they were out of view of the crowd. A strand of hair dropped across his forehead as he looked down at their joined hands. “Bailey, for months you’ve said we are just friends—good friends, but only friends.” He lifted her fingertips and rubbed a thumb across them. “I don’t have any other friends who let me hold their hand like this.”

Her breath caught on all that she couldn’t say.

He raised her hand to his lips and kissed her knuckles. “And I don’t have one solitary friend who would let me do that.” He kissed her hand once more, but slower. “I’m pretty sure that would get me punched by even my closest friends." A cheeky grin curved his mouth. "In fact, a few months ago you would have knocked me out if I had even attempted that."

"True." Her cheeks warmed despite the cool air blowing on them. Thank heavens it was dark out so he couldn't see her blush.

He didn't speak but only watched her eyes. She anticipated his next move with more giddiness than a kid on Christmas morning. She expected him to kiss her more or pull her close or declare his love, or hopefully all three.

He simply lowered her hand and let it go. "So what has changed?"

She wanted to stuff her fingertips back into his hand and bat her eyes like a swoony cartoon character. "Changed?"

"Between us?"

"Us?"

"Mm hm." He lowered his voice even though no one was around. "You let me touch you now, hold you even. Believe me, I like it, but when I wanted to kiss you last year, you said you weren't in the same place I was—that you didn't know if you would ever want to be more than friends. I swore I'd never make that mistake again. So I'm asking you straight out: has something changed between us?"

The skin along her arms tingled—whether from the chilly breeze or the pressure to be vulnerable, she couldn't tell. Their friendship was at stake; her heart was at stake. Both were worth protecting at any cost. She crossed her arms tightly for warmth and for security. "Rev, I…"

While she thought of what to say, he took off his coat and draped it over her shoulders. The heat that lingered in his jacket soaked into her skin.

Maybe this was what John had meant: two are better than one. The prospect of having someone to love and to love her back made the hard parts in life seem more bearable. If simply having him near brought her this much hope, she couldn't imagine what a lifelong relationship with him would bring.

Then again, judging by her past, if she found love, she would soon lose it. She'd known so many people who lost their true love during the water poisoning or the plague or the war. Yes, some people did indeed enjoy love for a lifetime, but it seemed most people only knew it for a short time. That was why she'd sworn her whole life that she wouldn't risk her heart—or her independence—to know true love at all.

Yet here she was, behind a barn under the moonlight with a man who adored her, the only man she would even consider. She looked down at the coat that topped her dress. "I don't know what to say."

He smoothed the coat sleeves over her shoulders and grinned. "It's customary to say *thank you.*"

"No, not for the coat. About your question. About us."

A depth returned to his eyes. "Am I right, though? Have your feelings—"

Before he could ask for the words she couldn't say, she raised her face to his and kissed him.

A jolt of surprise stopped his breath, but he quickly recovered and returned her kiss with more passion than she knew him capable of. He gently held her face with both hands. If anything was going to trigger her self-defense, it would have been that. Face held, lips covered, shoulders draped in a heavy coat.

But she wasn't afraid.

She wasn't trapped. She was here in this position with this man on her own desire. And there was no place else she'd rather be.

She pulled back and looked up at him, waiting for his usual rebuke when she'd broken some tradition.

He only smiled, his devoted eyes reflecting the passion flooding her heart. "I'll take that as a yes."

CHAPTER THIRTEEN

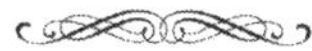

On the ride back to the Colburns' house after the barn dance, Bailey sat in the back of John's wagon on a wooden crate while Revel crouched nearby. He didn't speak but only held her fingertips loosely in his hand. Lydia sat on a hay bale opposite Bailey and cradled her sleeping little boy.

Scant moonbeams penetrated the wagon cover. It was enough light for Bailey to see Lydia's eyes move from Revel's hand to Bailey's face and back.

Bailey quickly looked away. If John knew she had feelings for Revel, and if Connor knew there was more than friendship brewing between them, surely Lydia knew too. Still, she pulled her fingertips out of his warm hand. Not that she was too immature to handle a public display of affection—though a mocking childhood voice sang in her head: *Bailey's got a boyfriend.* She simply wasn't ready to answer questions—not from Revel and certainly not from anyone else.

When they arrived at the house, she hopped out of the wagon without waiting for a man's courteous hand and held little Andrew while Lydia climbed down. They were already out by the time Connor climbed down from the front bench and rounded the wagon. He saw his wife standing on the ground, raised a surprised brow, and immediately looked at Bailey.

She could also feel Revel's gaze on her. Instead of looking at him, she met John at the front of the wagon, thanked him for the lovely evening, then let herself into the house.

As everyone entered the kitchen behind her, she said a general "Goodnight, all" to the group and continued walking to her bedroom. Opening one's heart didn't mean losing the ability to walk or open doors or climb down from wagon gates.

She prayed no one would knock on her door while she changed out of the dress she didn't completely despise wearing tonight. The gentle footfalls of Revel's gait passed her door as she removed the girly comb from her hair. He didn't knock. They all knew the house rules, and Revel had rules of his own. His gentlemanly manners were growing on her.

She waited for silence in the hallway before tiptoeing to the washroom. Once in bed and safe from everyone else's questions, she gave hers to the Lord and slipped into the kindest sleep she'd known in weeks.

Awakening to the full sun streaming into her window, her first thought was of Revel. Her lazy body lingered under the warm quilt while she traced the ceiling's shape with a fingertip—the very fingertip he'd held so sweetly on the wagon ride home last night. Now she couldn't remember why she'd let go.

John had said everyone could sleep in after the late night of dancing, but the aroma of pancakes and coffee seeped into her room and lured her from the bliss of lovely thoughts. Little feet thudded the floorboards upstairs, and Connor's muffled voice called out for

Andrew to *settle down* or *stop running* or some other overused parental command that had already become white noise to the spirited boy.

More voices murmured in the kitchen, so Bailey dressed and went out to greet the morning. As soon as she stepped into the kitchen, everyone stopped talking and looked across the room at her. Lydia and Sophia stood near the stove with fretful faces while John and Revel conferred near the open back door with their hands on their hips, their brows furrowed.

Everyone's eyes were fixed on her. She didn't expect them to be happy about her and Revel kissing if that's what this was about—and she dearly hoped he hadn't announced it with his morning greeting—but she didn't expect to be greeted with such serious and sad expressions either.

This couldn't be about her and Revel. She stopped at the table. "What's up, guys?"

Sophia's eyes were saucer wide, and her voice cracked as she spoke. "It was him. The outsider. He was in here last night." She pointed at the floor. "Look at the muddy footprints."

Bailey found a fingernail to bite. Sandy scuffs of dirt marked the waxed wooden planks, but they weren't exactly identifiable prints. She looked at John. "Those could have been from any of us last night. We all came in at the same time. I know I forgot to take my shoes off at the door."

He scratched his freshly trimmed beard. "A full loaf of bread and a dish of butter were taken."

Lydia pressed a hand to her middle. "And my last jar of blackberry jam."

Though Bailey's empty stomach sank with dread, she forced humor into her voice. "At least he has a discerning palate."

No one broke even the faintest of grins.

Sophia covered her quivering chin with nervous fingers. "Thank God I locked the cottage after Nicholas walked me home last night. I sleep out there all alone, you know."

John touched her shoulder with a fatherly hand. "You may sleep in the house if you are scared, Sophia."

Bailey glanced around the kitchen. Nothing else seemed out of place, and the dirty marks on the floor didn't go beyond the kitchen table. Since the intruder hadn't ventured farther into the house, he must have only come inside for food.

Or to test them.

And he'd found them an easy mark, a trusting home with an unlocked back door. Even she had slept soundly through it all. But she was awake now and with every heartbeat her blood warmed more and more.

Justin Mercer had been right. The Global guy had survived and was a threat to them all. Her muscles tightened and made it easy to ignore her hungry stomach. Fresh adrenaline awakened her system better than any cup of coffee could. She was ready to take care of business. "Has anyone checked outside yet?"

John shook his head. Revel still hadn't spoken. Sophia held both hands to her heart. "I didn't see anyone when I walked from the cottage to the house. But I didn't look around because I wasn't expecting him." She sucked in a quick breath. "He could have been watching me the whole time. He might be out there right now. He could be in the cottage!"

Kid giggles and tiny thuds rumbled upstairs. Connor was up there with his son, enjoying a lazy morning. For someone who used to be obsessed with keeping the Land safe, he didn't seem to care that an intruder—from Global no less—had been in his home while his family slept last night.

Bailey pointed at the ceiling and asked John, "Does Connor know about this?"

He shook his head again. "I am going up to speak with him now."

Revel remained at the doorway, staring blankly at the floor. While the others shakily prepared breakfast, Bailey walked over to him. He didn't reach for her or even make eye contact, so she spoke first. "Do you think it was Koslov?"

He heaved a breath then spoke, his morning voice an octave lower than it would be for the rest of the day. "Come with me."

She plucked her hiking boots from the shoe rack and followed him outside. As she crossed the threshold, Sophia said, "Please, close the door behind you."

Bailey glanced at Lydia for confirmation to close the always-open door. Lydia nodded rapidly.

Revel stayed a pace ahead of Bailey as she crossed the dirt driveway. He didn't check his surroundings for the intruder or scan the ground for clues while he marched past the cottage and toward the barn. Instead of being alert or even afraid, he seemed annoyed.

She did the scanning for them and doubled her steps to catch up to him. "Rev, where are we going?"

He lifted a finger to his lips for her to be quiet. Had he seen the Global guy out here? If so, why wasn't he waiting for Connor or carrying his crossbow?

The answers didn't matter if this meant she got to help him surprise attack the guy and take down Global. Her fists flexed and relaxed, warming up for a fight. It wouldn't be a long fight, nor a hard one, and those pancakes would taste even better after the victory.

Revel slowed his steps as he passed the closed barn doors and sneaked to the edge of the building. He crept around the corner, then his shoulders slumped and he spoke in a full voice. "Nothing. There's nothing back here at all. I thought for sure he would have left the…"

She scanned the paddock beyond the barn all the way to the forest path. There was no one in sight. The chickens were content, the horses calm. She shielded her eyes from the morning sun and surveyed the yard to the road in front of the property. "Why did you think he would leave something back here?"

His Adam's apple raised and lowered as he swallowed hard. "I should've said something a long time ago. Bailey, I wanted to tell you. Honestly."

The thin scars on her heart threatened to burst. "You wanted to tell me what?"

"But even more than tell you when it first happened, I wanted to settle the matter myself and then tell you when it was over." He toed the dirt with his boot. "I wanted to take care of something important instead of always having to go to Connor or John. I needed to handle something myself. Now I see how dumb it was of me."

She looked back at the house where Connor was exiting the back door. He was looking at the ground around the house, probably checking for footprints, but he would be up here within minutes, no doubt. "Revel, what's going on?"

He spotted Connor too, then returned his attention to her and reached for her hand. He held her fingertips loosely as he had last night, but now there was a faint quiver in his hand. "I want you to hear it from me first before I have to tell Connor and everyone, all right?"

"All right."

He rubbed the back of his neck with the other hand. "The day after Mercer arrived, I found a note from Koslov by the barn door saying he meant us no harm. Mercer had claimed the man would kill him, and I knew you wanted to hunt him down. Connor was certain he was already dead. No one agreed. So, I kept the note to myself and left food for him here," he pointed to the ground under the barn's eave, "and a note saying we could help him. The next day, the food was gone, so I left more food and some clothes from the rag pile. I thought of the blood that Connor and I found at the bluffs, so I left him gray leaf medicine and clear instructions because I figured English wasn't his first language. He took the food and the clothing, but the gray leaf medicine was untouched in the basket. That was the day I had to leave for the southern villages."

She remembered Revel in the kitchen with a basket that morning. She had joked about it and he'd seemed nervous. That reaction made sense now, but one thing didn't. "Why didn't you tell us before you left town? If you were providing his food, how did you expect him to survive while you were gone."

"I don't know."

"So that's why laundry went missing from the line and why Mrs. Foster said someone stole a whole pan of cobbler from her porch this week."

"I don't know."

"You don't know much, do you?" As soon as the words left her mouth, she regretted them.

He looked away from her as Connor approached from the house. "I already said I'm sorry for how I handled it. I wanted to impress you by taking charge of something important." He released her hand and stared at the ground. "Clearly, I'm not the man you deserve."

Half of her felt her best friend's pain and wanted to tell him not to give his mistake a second thought. The other half wanted to finish what Revel should have done three weeks ago. The safety of the women that she knew were frightened was far more important than her personal feelings for Revel. She took a step back too, and then another. "I can't do this right now."

She turned and marched toward the house. As she passed the cottage, Connor stopped her. "Did you find anything up there?"

"Nope. Nothing."

He folded his certain arms. "Sergei Koslov is dead. I don't know who came into the house for food last night, but it wasn't him."

"Oh, it was Global, all right." She pointed back at Revel, who was still standing under the barn's eave. "Go ask Revel. Apparently he and Koslov are BFFs."

She didn't wait for Connor to respond but continued to the house. A pancake breakfast while she formulated her plan would be a great way to power up for the battle. Since the men weren't doing their self-proclaimed duty to protect the Land and stop Global from killing them all in their sleep, it was up to her.

* * *

Even after Revel confessed the whole story to Connor, he couldn't bring himself to sit in the kitchen with everyone and eat breakfast. The back of his throat was tighter than a sunbaked saddle strap. He might never eat again. He didn't deserve to.

He didn't deserve John Colburn's hospitality or Connor's trust or Bailey's love. Only the road called to him. That was where he belonged.

But for some reason, he couldn't get himself to leave just yet.

He perambulated the property, walking the same path that he would have walked during his security shift if Mercer hadn't arrived that night during Bailey's watch. When all the commotion had started, he did everything he could to protect Bailey, but she didn't need him.

She never needed him.

And why should she?

He could barely take care of himself. His life was spent trading mail for another day's room-and-board until he rode to the next village. His work was barely worth a meal and a shower. He wasn't in charge of anything. He wasn't producing anything. He was of no importance.

That was why when he'd found the outsider's note, it seemed like the perfect opportunity to show everyone what he was capable of—more importantly, to show Bailey what he could do for her, for the Land. To prove to them all that he was a man who could handle difficult situations just as competently as Connor and John and even Bailey.

But he'd handled it badly.

The thin grass swished over his ankles near the southeast corner of the paddock as he passed the entrance to the forest between the Colburn property and the bluffs.

He'd heard noises down that path when Koslov had escaped the wreckage and wandered inland that night, but he'd never found out what it was.

That didn't matter anymore. Now, only the memory of finding that note played in his mind over and over. If only he'd taken it straight to Connor like he should have.

As he turned at the firepit and passed the chicken coop, John met him near the back of the cottage. "Did you find anything unusual out here?"

"No, sir."

"Are you all right?"

"No, sir."

John angled his head. "Connor told me what you did—about the stranger's note and giving him food and clothing."

If Revel were facing any other man, he would keep his mouth shut and walk on, but there was no walking away from John Colburn. He sank his hands into his pockets and rubbed the gold coin Connor had given him when they found the artifacts in the mountains last year. "I should have brought the note to you or Connor when I found it."

John only gazed at him.

Revel's empty heart ached more painfully than his empty stomach. "Don't you agree?"

"Connor doesn't believe it was from Mr. Koslov because he feels certain the man died shortly after arriving."

"Do you think he died?"

John shrugged. "I did not see the blood trailing over the cliff or the tide blocking the caves below, but I trust Connor's judgment. I also did not see the note you found, but if you felt you needed to feed and clothe a person, I trust your judgement too."

Revel pointed at the coop's laying box, which was empty of eggs again this morning. "Well, I didn't succeed because he is hiding out and stealing from you."

"For sustenance."

"It's still wrong."

"Wrong but forgivable."

Revel couldn't see inside the open kitchen door from across the property. "Is Bailey helping Lydia clean up from breakfast?"

John nodded.

"She's probably plotting how she might protect the girls from Koslov."

John simply watched him with those sky-blue eyes.

Revel found the dirt in front of his boots easier to look at. "I only wanted to show her I could protect her, but all I did was send her into another fight. Just when things were looking… promising."

"Between you and Bailey?"

He met John's knowing gaze. "We kissed last night at the Fosters' party."

A half grin lightened John's expression.

"But I ruined everything. She's angry with me now." He thought about her biting tone. "Worse than angry—she's disappointed. And rightly so. I should have told her the truth about Koslov from the beginning. I apologized, but it didn't do any good." A shadow moved past the kitchen windows. He could tell who it was from this distance. "After the girls are done in the kitchen. I'll pack up and clear out."

John gave his shoulder a fatherly squeeze. "It would take more courage to wait on the Lord than to leave."

"Thanks, John, but you don't want me around here. Sophia and Lydia are both scared, and that's going it irritate Connor and make Bailey stay on guard. We both know it will be easier to handle this mess without me here."

"Easier for whom?"

Though he thought he was certain, his words came out as a question. "For you?"

John shook his head.

Revel felt like a child. "For me?"

John nodded. "That is why you should stay."

"And do what?"

"Take your eyes off yourself and look to Christ." John's tone took on the fullness it had during his sermons, yet his low volume kept his message private. "You need to rehearse God's faithfulness in your life. How has He helped you? Saved you? Protected you? Provided for you? As you worshipfully recount His good deeds, your trust in Him will grow."

He made it sound so easy. As if trusting God was the answer to everything.

Revel glanced in the direction of the shore where he first encountered Bailey Colburn of America—even if it was by shooting her. Then he looked at the house where they had enjoyed long conversations and connected in a deeper way than he knew was possible. Then his gaze moved to the barn where Bailey had walked away from him in disappointment moments ago.

Blaze was inside that barn, waiting for his oats. Revel could have his horse fed and saddled and be on the road in less than an hour. This wasn't about trusting God. This was about acknowledging his limitations and getting out of the village before he made more mistakes.

He squared his shoulders. “Thanks for the advice, John. I’ll think about it.”

CHAPTER FOURTEEN

Bailey didn't talk while she helped Lydia and Sophia clear the breakfast table and wash dishes. The other women had plenty to say, so she simply listened, not to the words but to the panic that fueled their conversation.

Sophia asked one what-if question after another, then answered herself with another fear-filled question. Before the dishes were dry, Lydia started giving credence to Sophia's concerns. The doctor chattered while she swept the pantry floor with nervous strokes. "I know my husband firmly insists there is no way Mr. Koslov survived, but without finding the remains, there is no proof. You're right, Sophia. It is frightening to think that man could be outside right now."

Sophia glared at the window. "He is probably waiting to catch one of us alone so he can pounce like a ravenous beast."

Bailey hung the tea towel over the empty dish rack with the same calm she used to feel before a sparring match with a stronger opponent. Sophia continued with no sign of stopping, so Bailey had to interrupt. "I think I'll go for a walk this morning… a nice long walk on the beach. I probably won't be back before lunch."

Lydia reversed out of the pantry with widened eyes. "Aren't you concerned about the stranger being out there?"

Bailey ignored the question and asked one of her own. "When I was at the elder meeting, one man mentioned old fishing shacks down the coast about two miles. He hadn't been since he was a boy and didn't know if they were still standing. Have either of you ever seen them?"

The change of subject snapped Sophia to attention. "Who would want to go see old fishing shacks?"

Lydia shook her head. "I wouldn't want to. Levi and some of his school friends went once. They planned to stay a few nights and fish. Levi hated it. He said the shacks were barely standing and he wasn't about to fix them while the others fished, so he left. And then the tide came back in and so he couldn't walk home along the shore. He had to go the long way around through the forest and over the bluffs." She almost smiled at the memory. "He was so angry by the time he got home. Then again, he was always upset about something at that age."

She paused, then her face changed and she gaped at Bailey. "Is that where you think Mr. Koslov has been living?"

Bailey shrugged. "I was just curious. I feel like going for a walk and want to see something I haven't seen here yet."

Lydia inched forward. "You aren't thinking of going down to the shacks by yourself, are you?"

When Bailey didn't immediately respond, Sophia spun to face her. The delicate chignon on top of her head wobbled. "Bailey, you mustn't go! What if he is out there?"

No wonder Connor insisted the Global guy was dead. He probably preferred letting an enemy steal his clothes and dinner rather than listening to these two needle away at their own nerves.

She kept her tone between placating and patronizing. "Listen ladies, I'm going for a walk. I will be fine."

Sophia stiffened. "But what if he attacks you?"

"Then you and Lydia can stitch him up later."

Neither woman responded, so Bailey grinned as she backed out of the kitchen. "That was just a joke. Don't worry about me. Everything will be okay." She pointed at the back door. "Do you want this closed?"

Lydia nodded slowly, broom handle still locked in her white knuckles.

Bailey dropped the grin as soon as she was outside the house. She would not murder a man, but she would use lethal force to defend herself. If the Global guy saw her alone, he would try to grab her. She knew his type—no matter what continent he was born on. If he saw her alone, he would think she was defenseless and try to take advantage of the situation. It happened all the time in the outside world. If she could help it, it would never happen in the Land.

She would let him catch her. Then with two quick moves she would free herself and stop his heart, and free the women from their fear and the Land from Global's threat.

Men's voices murmured behind the medical cottage. It sounded like John and Revel were talking, so she took the other path from the house to the beach. It didn't matter which way she went to get past the bluffs; she knew where the Global guy was hiding.

Morning sunlight splintered between the pine trees as she hiked through the woods. The sand deepened when she left the forest and reached the shore. She paused by the cairn of stones the Founders had built when they came to the Land. The incline by the cairn was the perfect place to look out at the ocean.

Though the sky overhead was clear, a distinct line of haze smudged the horizon.

Great.

Justin had been right on both counts: Koslov was still alive and the volcanic ash cloud was covering the globe.

She forced herself to look away from the ghostly haze that hung low on the horizon over the ocean, encircling the Land as far as she could see. She couldn't do anything about that right now, and next year's weather wouldn't matter if one of Global's trained pawns systematically killed them all in their sleep.

At least that was what Lydia and Sophia were convinced would happen. And they might be right. He might try to kill them or expose the Land to Global.

But not if she stopped him first.

She hiked south toward the bluffs where she'd found Justin that night. The water line was out the farthest she'd ever seen it, leaving the ocean's regurgitated seaweed clumps and washed-up surprises on the sand between the rocky shore and the cliffs above.

She stood still and listened to the waves for a moment. The tide was still going out. She had plenty of time to pass the caves that were sealed off whenever the tide was in. That was where Connor thought the Global guy had been trapped and drowned, but on his few and flimsy searches, he never found any hard evidence.

No surprise. People didn't stay down here long for fear of the tide's swift return.

It wasn't the tide's return that tingled her spine, but the eerie hum of the waves and the rocks. If she had the right equipment, she would love to measure the magnetic resonance here. Somehow it all had to play into the anomaly that hid the Land.

Whatever it was, it was creepy.

So was the stench.

Why must there always be dead creatures washed up on a beach after a tide went out? No matter where she was in the world, it seemed every good beach hike was marred by some rotten scent. Every step she took was faster than the one before.

She covered her nose with her sweatshirt sleeve and found a path of solidly packed sand to walk on. There wasn't a solitary footprint anywhere. The Global guy wasn't in those caves. Since items had gone missing in the village for a few days and then nothing happened for a few days, he was obviously living somewhere past the caves and out of sight of the bluffs above.

She glanced from one cave and crevice to the next then to the bluffs above, then behind her as she hurried up the shoreline to the tall, marsh grass where she and Revel had found Tim's life vest and hat last year.

Seagulls scurried out of her way as she came to the grassy area between the sand and the bluffs. A dark lump near the grass caught her eye, so she stopped. The smell intensified as she inched closer. Sunlight glinted off the slimy object: a dead cuttlefish, probably twenty pounds when alive. Disgusted, she backed away from the grass and kept marching along the shore past the bluffs.

On many occasions she'd hiked to those bluffs from the other side and stood atop the cliffs to stare out at the ocean, thanking God for saving her from the warring outside world and bringing her safely to the Land.

She loved this place and these innocent people and would do anything to defend them, even if Connor wouldn't. She'd once despised him for acting like the gatekeeper of a place that wasn't his to guard. Now he didn't seem concerned about his family's safety here. It was up to her to protect them. She wouldn't wait around while Global took another innocent life.

She kept trekking forward along the hard-packed sand. Ahead, the cliffs squeezed close to the water's edge—close enough she couldn't see what was beyond them. For now, the tide was out far enough there was still a dry path between the water and the rock wall. That path probably led to the old fishing shacks. The Global guy had to be hiding out there.

Had Connor and his little search crew even checked this far? Nope. They assumed the Global guy went over the cliff and didn't survive.

Well, she would do the job they should have done weeks ago. More than locate the man, she would end his little game.

All at once, she heard the unfaithfulness of her thoughts. How could she praise God one moment for bringing her to the Land and then plot how she would kill a man the next?

Where was her meekness? Her mercy? Her reflection of the grace God had shown her?

Even as her spirit screamed for her to stop, her feet kept going forward. There was a threat to people she loved, helpless women she had to protect. She had to be proactive and take care of the problem. That's what she was good at—taking care of problems.

To her flesh it felt right. To her spirit… not so much.

She'd come to Good Springs this autumn to learn from John Colburn. If he were here beside her right now, he would say it takes more courage to wait on the Lord than to take matters into our own hands. He would quote a scripture verse, maybe several. She could think of several herself that applied to the situation, thanks to the memory work he'd assigned her.

Wait for the Lord. Be strong and let your heart take courage. Yes, wait for the Lord.

The battle is not yours but God's.

But she always took matters into her own hands. That's how she survived. That was how she was bold, how she was courageous.

And yet, she didn't want to live like that anymore, especially in her new life in the Land.

She stopped, ignoring the cold rocky wall to her right and the roar of the waves to her left, and looked up to the clear sky above. "Lord, I know You are just as much in me as You are up there. I have the strength and desire to protect the people who need me. But I need You. Give me the courage to do what is right in Your eyes, not mine."

Her feet continued moving forward, but her mind went back to all that the Lord had done in her life. He had turned her ashes into beauty. He always took care of her, just as he would take care of Lydia and Sophia and the rest of them. He had put gracious people in her life here, people who loved her, people she should listen to.

As she rounded the rocks, the view down the coast became clear. Just inland where the woods met the windswept sand, the splintered roof of a dilapidated fishing shack leaned against an old pine tree.

* * *

Revel flopped his new mailbag onto the quilted bed in the Colburns' guest room. He'd only used the bag for a couple of weeks and already it was loosening up, its thick leather conforming to his use, its sturdy straps to his body. What a shame he had to leave Bailey just when they were beginning to conform to each other in new ways. She was finally getting used to his touch, no longer stiffening or moving away from him. She even let him lead their dance last night, their bodies moving effortlessly as one.

And then she'd kissed him.

But that was over now. He couldn't waste time thinking about what might have been if he'd done things differently. There would be plenty of time for regrets on the road back to Falls Creek.

He rolled his clothes and stuffed them into his old satchel. It wouldn't be so bad out there on the road alone. He enjoyed his job—most of the time. His thumb traced the buckle on the mailbag that was custom made for him, traded for a job well done—proof his work mattered to some people. It wasn't just a way to stay unfettered by a home and family. His courier service was necessary to the Land. His choice of professions had been blessed by his father and John and Connor. He had to remember that or he would fall prey to old lies.

Maybe that was what John meant by rehearsing God's provision in his life.

He withdrew a stack of envelopes from the mailbag's front pocket—mostly messages awaiting delivery. The first was a letter from his aunt to his mother. Traveling to Riverside every other week had given him the chance to get to spend time with his mother and heal their relationship. God had certainly helped him there.

Other notes were from the northern villages for the southern villages about the crop suggestions in preparing for the possible long winter. God was using him for meaningful work. That was something he'd always prayed for.

His courier service wasn't only convenient for the people, it was part of the Land's security. And it wasn't simply his livelihood. He had worked with Connor to deliver security messages and with the overseers to deliver important community decisions. Even during the past three weeks, he and Bailey had worked together for the Land. She used her knowledge to help prepare the crop suggestions and he delivered that important information to every village.

They worked well together no matter what they did—stacking hay, weeding gardens, escorting travelers across the Land. They were better together.

They belonged together.

Somehow.

He couldn't know what a future with her would look like, but he yearned for it. Would he build them a house on the property his father left him at Falls Creek? Would she even want a home of her own or would she want to live at the inn with people while he was traveling? Would he have to stop his courier service and stay at Falls Creek with her? Maybe she would want to join him on the road.

The details didn't matter to him. He would do whatever it took to spend his life with her. They had already endured so much together. And they could face anything that came… if only she would give him a chance.

That was it. He had to stop waiting for her to give him a chance, to listen to him, to get used to him. He had allowed her to direct their relationship for long enough. She loved him too. Last night proved it. So what if he'd made yet another mistake? He could make amends. If they were going to be together, he would probably spend a lot of his time making amends with her.

And that started now.

He left his bags where they were on the bed, but stuffed the letters back into his mailbag for safe keeping. As the stack of messages slid into the front pocket, one folded paper caught his eye. It was a note from the boy Teddy Vestal's parents, describing him, begging the overseers of the Land to send him home if they found him. Revel had shown it to every overseer so they might all be on the lookout for the runaway. So far, no one had seen the young man.

Revel thought of the missing food and clothing and eggs. He considered the sneakiness of the thief, but also the benign way he operated. And the sloppily written note on the ground by the barn that day: I mean no harm. Give food please.

Revel stuffed the folded note with Teddy Vestal's description into his satchel then glanced out the window. Two willow trees swayed in the breeze by the clothesline.

He needed to speak to Bailey at once. He rushed out of the guestroom and down the hallway where he knocked on Bailey's door.

No answer.

The parlor was empty, but Sophia and Lydia were in the kitchen at the table, whispering.

"Pardon my interruption, ladies. Do either of you know where Bailey is?"

The women exchanged a fretful glance but neither spoke for a several seconds. Finally, Lydia lifted her chin at him. "She said she was going for a walk down the shore, past the bluffs. Left half an hour ago."

The trepidation in Lydia's voice made sense, but he had to confirm it for himself. "Is she searching for the intruder?"

Lydia nodded rigidly. "We couldn't stop her."

Sophia's bottom lip quivered, so he gave her shoulder a brotherly squeeze. "Don't be afraid, ladies. Bailey can protect herself, though I doubt very much that she is in danger—at least not the sort you are imagining."

Before they could question him, he dashed out the back door.

Bailey might be at the shore hunting for the person who had sneaked into the Colburns' house last night. Whether she was right or wrong to do so, he couldn't say. But of one thing he was certain: She was looking for the wrong person.

* * *

Bailey crept toward the slanted fishing shack that cowered in the grass between the sandy beach and the shaded woods. The shack's hodgepodge boards looked about as sturdy as kindergarten craft sticks. A few yards away, the ruins of another shack huddled in the trees, and another farther down from that. From where she stood, only one shack still stood.

Dead seedlings poked out of its slipping roof shingles. Its door was closed and the rope handle pulled to the outside. A smattering of muddy footprints carved a path through the mossy ground from the woods to the shack. Whoever had made that path wasn't home at the moment.

She studied the footprints and the ground around her. She hadn't seen any prints on the path she took from the shore. After glancing around, she squatted by one dirt outline. The shoe that made this print didn't have tread lines—not like shoes from the outside world. It was a boot print, much like the men's boots here, but narrower. The women's work shoes in the Land had a thinner heel than then men's boots. She stood upright and wiggled her toes, thankful for her well-soled hiking boots.

This was certainly a man's print, but a small one. Maybe something had happened to Koslov's shoes and these boots were all he could steal. Some adolescent boy in the village was probably walking barefoot to school right now.

The sandy path she'd taken from the shore was clear. In the opposite direction, a buck stood at the forest edge about a hundred feet away. The deer would run if someone came from that way.

She checked the bushes in all directions, listened to the birds, the waves, the wind. Certain she was alone, she inched toward the shack, hands taut and ready to strike.

Neither window had glass or curtains only splintery shutters. The shutters on the little window on the front were closed, but the window on the sea side was open.

She peered inside.

Empty.

She tugged on the door's rope handle, but it didn't open. Pushing didn't work either. She glanced around once more, then yanked the rope away from the doorframe. When something inside clicked, she sent a determined shoulder into the door and it swung open, clattering the unstable walls.

A bed of stacked horse blankets and stained towels covered the dirt floor in the shack's corner. The makeshift bed seemed cramped at maybe five foot long, but she'd slept in worse conditions as a child. An oil lantern waited next to the bed. The Colburns' butter dish, a cup, a flask, and half a loaf of yesterday's bread were crammed on an overturned crate the resident used for a table.

A row of grimy glass jars lined the wall between the bed and the crate. Seashells filled one jar. The other held fishhooks and bobbers, and the last had an assortment of rocks and shells. A few loose marbles were arranged in a colorful circle beside the jar.

The shack's small-footed occupant seemed unusual for the Land, but he was no Russian hockey player who'd been drafted into military service for Global.

She left everything as she found it and pulled the door closed behind her while she stepped out of the shack.

Maybe someone still came down here for a respite of solitary fishing like the elders had said they did long ago. But if the current resident was here to fish, why would he need to steal food from the village every few days? And clothing?

It didn't make sense, but it wasn't the reason she came. She had found a possible hideout, but she hadn't found the Global guy.

As soon as her feet left the grass around the shack and hit the sand, she heard a change in the waves' rhythm. The tide was turning and would soon block her path. If she was going to return the way she came, she needed to keep moving to cover the two mile trek.

The breeze coming in from the water hit the rock wall as she reached the bluffs. The cliffs towered above her, pulling her attention up when it should have been forward. Connor and Revel claimed the blood trail on top of those cliffs was proof the Global guy had died while trying to climb down. But that was three weeks ago and there was still no sign of his remains. Maybe Connor was right and the body had been swept out to sea.

As she neared the marshy area where she'd found the dead cuttlefish, she lifted her collar over her nose to mask the smell. It didn't help.

She scanned the ground from the ocean to her right, to the beach in front of her where it was narrowed by more cliffs, and then to tall grass to her left. The dark lump of the bloated cuttlefish still gleamed in the sunlight. Gross.

As her gaze darted away, something else claimed her attention. Something larger. A shadow in the grass that extended beyond the dead fish.

Her feet stopped. Her heart rate increased. It was probably just driftwood, but the last time she saw something hiding, it had been Justin Mercer. She had to check it out.

The stench intensified the closer she moved toward the waist-high grass. She studied the dark shape along the ground beyond the edge of the grass. Maybe it was a dead deer. Or some big sea creature that had washed in days ago. It seemed too flat to be a whale, too long to be a turtle.

She tried not to look at the icky cuttlefish as she leaned over it to get a better look into the tall grass. Her foot glided forward to give her another few inches of reach. As she shifted her weight to her toes, she felt a lump under foot and snapped back.

It was a man's hand, gray and laced with seaweed.

Her eyes followed the hand to the forearm where a tattoo of a bear marked the decaying skin, then up the soaked black sleeve to the man's shoulder where a mildewed Global patch had lost its self-granted glory.

She backed away with both hands over her nose and mouth, a wave of nausea threatening her usually strong stomach. Deep sand shifted under her feet, wobbling her balance. All she could hear was her own pulse.

The girls were right: she shouldn't have come here. Not alone. She should have accepted Revel's apology and suggested they work together. He should be here now. With her. She needed him.

She kept backing up until the hard-packed sand was under foot, then she spun toward the ocean, tasting bile.

She tried to focus on the horizon to clear her head, but the distant ring of haze only sullied the view. With her hands fastened to her knees, she let the salty breeze hit her face while she stabilized her breathing. Champions didn't get woozy. Fighters didn't gag when they found a corpse.

No, but humans did.

And humans needed each other. She wasn't meant to be alone. Not now, and not in life.

The ocean air flushed the putrid scent molecules out of her sinuses. She would have given anything to sniff some gray leaf. All she had was ocean air and her own resolve.

Breathe in, breathe out. Slowly.

She felt more like an inexperienced yellow belt in her first real match rather than a world-ranked black belt, hardened by an upbringing in the foster system.

How had she gotten so soft?

It was the Land. It was the innocence of its culture, the charm of its simplicity, the beauty of its unadulterated landscape.

But her vulnerability came from more than conforming to her new life in the Land. It was from the sweetness of allowing herself to be loved… and to love. She loved the people here. They'd become her friends, her mentors, her family.

And then there was Revel.

He was all those things to her and more. So much more.

Her stomach settled, but her nerves remained shaky. She still wasn't completely in control nor would she be so long as she was in love.

In love?

In the midst of a disturbing situation, all she could think of was the bulging feelings in her that she didn't know what to do with. She made a great fighter, but a lousy girlfriend.

She should be swoony in a happy way, not sick to her stomach, right? At least that was how the movies showcased being in love.

Her feelings for Revel went beyond friendship, beyond attraction, beyond anticipation. The way she'd felt about him wasn't like in those movies, but it was certainly love.

The steady beat of footsteps approached from behind.

She didn't need to turn around; she knew that gait. Even when he was hurrying toward her, she knew how he moved and anticipated his touch.

Revel gently laid his warm palm across her back. "Are you all right?"

She continued drawing long inhales of the fresh ocean air, wishing he wouldn't see her like this as much as she wished he would stay close. "No."

He gave the air two short sniffs. "What's that smell?"

"Sergei Koslov."

"Dead?"

"Oh, yeah. Has been for a while. Probably washed in with the tide."

Revel's comforting hand rubbed her back. "I'm sorry you were the one to find him. No wonder you're in such a state."

Her spine straightened. "I once saw a competitor's leg get snapped so badly the bone poked through his tournament uniform. I watched my friends succumb to the plague. I held my roommate's hand while she died from the water poisoning." She pointed at the dark smudge in the grassy area behind them. "That I can handle."

He gave her a disbelieving look.

"Okay, fine. I can handle it as soon as I get the smell out of my brain. But that's not what's wrong with me."

His voice was as gentle as his touch. "So what is wrong then?"

"It's this." She waved a finger between them. "This is too much for me to handle."

Everything in her wanted to pour her heart out, to tell him she loved him, that she needed him now and always. That was the stupidest thing a woman could do these days. Yet the words burned on her tongue. If she told him, she would be forever changed. Love was so illogical. She couldn't explain her feelings. She took a step back.

He stopped her with a soft grip on her arm. "Bailey, wait. Don't walk away. Not again."

"I can't deal with this. I can't explain myself or what's happening inside me. I'm a scientist. Give me something I can rationalize." She flicked a glance toward the corpse. "I can understand that, but I can't understand what I'm feeling for you."

Patient resolve solidified his voice. "Good."

"What?"

"That's good. You're finally admitting your feelings for me." The sunlight hit his eyes, sending golden flecks through his hazel irises. "Do you know why I came out here?"

She sensed humor in his question, but nothing—not even her best friend—could make her laugh right now. "Because you're an over-protective but charming gentlemen who thought I needed to be rescued."

He shook his head and with a light touch to the small of her back ushered her along the shore and away from the stench. "Because you were right."

"I was?"

"You said that I don't know what I'm doing, and you were right. I don't know what I'm doing most of the time.

Never have. I make up life as I go and make my share of mistakes because of it. Always will."

"Rev, you don't—"

"No, listen. I'll always try my best to do right, but I will mess up. Often. But I'll keep apologizing. It's who I am."

They passed the rounded curve of the bluffs, putting the ugliness of death behind them. She looked at his profile as they ambled between the water and the rocks. "I like who you are."

"Thanks." He kept his hand on her back. "And you don't have to explain yourself to me. I already understand you."

Being understood *and* being loved. That was what was so overwhelming. She reached for his hand and held it, peace settling her heart. "I know you do."

"Good." He laced his fingers with hers and kept walking but gave her a half-grin. "You know what else? Connor was right about Koslov, but you were right about there being someone out here that we need to find. He is harmless, though. It's the runaway kid from Riverside, Teddy Vestal."

She stopped walking and let her fingers dangle in his strong hand. "That explains his little set up in the shack."

"Don't worry about him right now or the corpse or anything else. I'll get some of the guys and we'll handle all of that later. You did your work for the day. All right?"

He was correct: this was no longer her duty. Maybe it never had been. But it was time for her to let go. "All right."

He inched closer and looked down at her with a confidence that gave her a jolt. "And just so you have no doubt… I will always try to protect you whether you need me to or not."

She playfully poked a finger to his chest. "Fine. Just try not to get yourself killed trying to keep up with me."

He shrugged. "I only get one life, Bailey. I want to live it with you." The edge of his mouth curved. "Trying to keep up with you will probably be the death of me."

That got a smile out of her. "Wow, you really do understand me."

"I'd like to think so."

She looked up at him, her heart opening as she saw him for all he truly was. "And just so you know, I do need you."

"You have me." He lowered his lips to hers, connecting sweetly, privately in the way only he was allowed to, leaving no doubt in her mind that he was the answer to the question that drove her here weeks ago.

CHAPTER FIFTEEN

Revel led Blaze from the paddock to the Colburns' barn and tied his rope to the pole under the eave. The horse pulled against the line and snorted. Revel gave him a comforting stroke. "I wouldn't want to go back into the barn on such a fine day either. Wait here, boy. I'll be right back to clean your hooves."

Blaze snorted again and turned one horsey eye toward him.

Revel patted his velvety neck. "And a bucket of oats."

While he was in the tack room selecting a pick and a file, a series of clicks and clanks came from Connor's workroom. Blaze stood calmly outside the barn doors, so Revel walked toward the back of the barn. "Connor?"

"In here."

Before he reached the workroom, Connor leaned out of the door, ever vigilant about who knew what was inside the musty storage room. When Connor saw Revel was alone, he made space in the doorway. "Come in. What's up?"

Revel tapped the iron file and hoof pick together in a rapid rhythm that matched his nerves. "Nothing. Well, it's just that I didn't get to speak to you alone yesterday after… everything."

Connor rounded the worktable and covered his radio equipment with a drop cloth. He gave Revel a quick smirk before sitting on an overturned bucket. “Yeah, it looked like you and Bailey needed time together—alone.”

The afternoon Revel had spent in the Colburns’ parlor talking with Bailey—and simply listening to her voice—had been some of the sweetest hours of his life. A warm surge settled his heart. “We did. You were right last year when you said she wasn’t the marrying type, but she has changed. I’ve changed. Probably not as much as I want to, but I’m working on it. That’s what I wanted to talk to you about—to apologize for.”

Connor leveled his gaze on him. “Look Revel, you did what you thought was best. It would have been a bad idea to keep it from us if Koslov really had been alive, but since he wasn’t, I’m not worried about it.”

“Well, I am. I want to be a man you can trust, and what I did was wrong.” Revel’s voice tightened. “I thought I needed to prove I could take charge of something.”

“To whom?”

“Pardon?”

“You needed to prove yourself to whom?”

It felt like a trick question, but he knew Connor had a point to make. “I don’t know… to you. To John.”

“To yourself?”

“Maybe.”

“To your father?”

Revel’s breath caught in his lungs. Even though Connor had seemed busy with his overseer training and his family and his chores around the property, he still had been observing and judging everything that went on in his home—even with the people who were just passing through.

Revel slid the pick and file into his back pocket, no longer needing to fidget with them. "Yes, I wanted to be a man my father would have been proud of."

Connor's gaze didn't relent. "And Bailey?"

"And Bailey. Most of all Bailey. I wanted her to see me handle something big."

"If you plan on spending your life with her, you'll need to be able to handle big trouble." His smirk returned. "She certainly knows how to handle you."

For years, Revel had watched his friends get tamed by the women they loved. One by one they succumbed to committed relationships and pretended to complain about losing their freedom, but their pride in being chosen was thinly veiled.

For once Revel got to be that man.

He'd waited an eternity for this and wouldn't dare pretend that being chosen by Bailey was anything less than pure joy. A smile tugged at his lips. "She is my perfect match in every way."

Connor stuck out his fist. "Congrats, man."

He bumped Connor's fist. "Thank you." Maybe one day it would be as easy to forgive himself as it was for others to forgive him.

He left Connor in the workroom and walked through the dim barn, looking in each horse stall as he passed. He stopped at the stall where Bailey's horse was poking her head over the gate. "You waiting for your girl?" He petted Gee for a moment. "She'll be here to take care of you in a little while."

Something moved in the back corner of the stall, swishing the hay on the floor. At first, Revel thought he'd caught Gee's tail movement in his peripheral vision, but then the shadow moved again. He couldn't make out the shape, so he pushed Gee back from the gate and stepped into the stall.

The hunched figure stood up straight, revealing an adolescent boy. "I'm sorry, sir. Please don't hurt me."

"I won't hurt you." Revel halted where he was, blocking the stall's only exit with one hand and blocking Bailey's horse with the other. "Who are you?"

The young man wore one of Connor's shirts and the trousers Revel thought he'd given to Koslov. He stepped forward, his face grimy, his stringy hair dotted with bits of hay. "I'm nobody. Just needed a place to sleep, sir."

"Teddy Vestal?"

The boy's eyes widened, scant light making the whites seem bright. "How did you know my name?"

"Because I've been taking your parents' message to every village in the Land. They are worried sick about you. Especially your mother."

"She is?" He looked down at the hay-strewn floor. "I didn't mean to upset her. I just needed one of my adventures. They didn't seem to mind before. This is the first time I made it all the way to Good Springs. Just wanted to see the ocean, sir. I didn't think they'd miss me on account of having so many of us."

"You have a lot of siblings?"

"Three brothers and two sisters. I'm not the youngest, but I'm the smallest of the boys. No use to my father at all." His voice cracked. "I'm definitely not the favorite."

Revel knew the feeling. "Well, right now your parents want to see you more than anyone else on earth. Your mother is begging every trader in the Land to look for you."

"I only wanted to have some fun on my own. I didn't mean no harm."

"So you said in the note you left for me. That was you, wasn't it?"

Teddy met his gaze. "Yes, sir. I saw everyone here running around, searching for me that night, looking mean. I thought I was in for a pounding if they caught me. Especially that short-haired lady who's real quick."

The description of Bailey almost made Revel laugh. "Yeah, she's real quick. Real concerned about you too. She found your hideout yesterday."

"She did?"

"Yep. She went looking for you after you broke into the house the other night."

He shook his head rapidly and specks of hay fell from his hair. "I didn't break in—not like a robber or anything. The door was unlocked, so I went in to get food. The fish weren't biting. Or maybe my line is too short. I'm not sure, but I was getting hungry."

"You can't steal from people like that. You frightened the ladies who live here."

"I'm sorry."

"You should tell them yourself." He moved back to the doorway to give the boy space. "It's time to end this adventure. Let's go to the house so you can get cleaned up."

As the boy took a hesitant step forward, Connor came out of his workroom. "What's going on?"

Revel backed out of the stall so Connor could see the boy. "I just made a new friend. We've had correspondence and finally get to meet in person." He looked at the young man. "My name's Revel Roberts, by the way. Teddy, I'd like you to meet Connor Bradshaw. Connor, this is Teddy Vestal."

Connor thrust out his hand. "Good to meet you, Teddy. Nice t-shirt."

"Um…" Teddy looked down at the shirt he was wearing. "Is this yours?"

When Connor nodded, the boy frowned. "Oh. Sorry about that. My clothes got muddy."

Connor crossed his arms and gave Teddy a once over. "You can take the shirt home with you. But you definitely need clean clothes for now." He gave Revel a stiff thump on the shoulder. "Revel can see to that. He enjoys handling things, don't you, Rev?"

"Yeah, sure do." Revel chuckled as Connor returned to his workroom. Then he lifted his chin at the boy. "Come with me to the house. How old are you?"

"Fourteen next month."

"Fourteen, huh? That's about how old I was when I wanted the traders to take me with them on the road."

Teddy looked up at him while they left the barn. "Did you ever go on adventures?"

"Yes. Still do. I'm a courier now."

"That sounds like more fun than staying by yourself in an old fishing shack."

"Didn't like it?"

"I missed having someone to talk to."

"If you are hiding from people, you'll get lonely. I've learned that the hard way. Also, if you find yourself feeling lonely, you're probably hiding." Revel patted Blaze as they passed the horse. "And so after you get a long bath and a hot meal and a good night's sleep in a real bed, you can ride home with us tomorrow."

"Us?"

"Me and Bailey."

"That's the short-haired lady, huh? I saw you and her walking on the beach yesterday."

Revel wondered if the boy also saw them kiss, but he wasn't going to ask. "Wait here for a minute." He pointed at the threshold as he stepped into the kitchen's open back door. "Bailey? Lydia?"

Sophia stepped into the kitchen from the parlor first with Lydia close behind her. The doctor was holding her drowsy toddler, who had just awoken from his afternoon nap.

Sophia looked at the young man standing in the doorway. "Does someone need medical attention?"

Revel put a hand on Teddy's shoulder. "No, just a bath and clean clothes. This is our intruder."

Sophia and Lydia exchanged a look as the boy fumbled an apology from where he stood at the threshold.

Bailey walked into the kitchen from the parlor. She grinned at Teddy. "Did you bring back Mr. Colburn's favorite butter dish?"

Teddy glanced frantically at all of them. "Um, no."

Bailey cut between the other women, skirted Revel, and ushered the boy inside with a gentle hand. "Come on in and get washed up. Oh, but leave your shoes at the door this time."

Revel stayed at the door and watched with amazement along with Lydia and Sophia. Bailey walked Teddy to the sink. She stood on the pedal beneath to start the water flow and made him scrub his dirt-caked hands. Her blend of humor and authority had the young man divided between staring at her and following her instructions.

Revel watched her with a delight that crowded out every last bit of hesitancy in his heart. He'd never seen her pay much attention to children, but in minutes she'd taken to this teenaged runaway as if she'd done this her whole life. And he understood why.

It was simply one more way that she was his perfect match, and he hers.

* * *

Bailey kept an eye on the staircase as she sank into the comfy sofa in the Colburns' living room. She let out a long breath after a full day of preparing to leave Good Springs tomorrow. As she emptied her lungs of air, her mind relaxed, allowing her to feel the fullness of her heart and the warmth of the fireplace.

When she had left Falls Creek, her only desire had been to come here and sit in this very room and learn deeper truths from John Colburn—truth about God and life and maybe about the nagging yearning she couldn't articulate.

John shifted in his armchair and peered at her over his Bible. His silver eyebrows raised with fatherly curiosity. "Is the young man asleep?"

She nodded and pointed up to where Teddy Vestal was in the spare bedroom upstairs, draped across what had to be the most comfortable bed he had ever slept on. "Do you think he will still be here in the morning?"

John lowered his Bible to his lap. "I think the only trouble you will have with that young man is dragging him out of bed to leave with you tomorrow. Then again, he seemed to take a liking to you and to Revel. Once he awakens, he will be at your heels." He lifted an emphatic finger. "Once he awakens."

"Yeah, I'm sure you're right." She thought back to her life at that age. "I remember when I was between foster homes and sometimes I'd get to sleep over at a friend's house—anyone from my martial arts team who had sane parents and a sturdy roof. I would sleep so hard for as long as they would let me." She glanced up at the crossbeams in the ceiling. "Teddy could use the extra sleep. It's a shame we have to leave here so early."

"What time are you and Revel meeting the trader?"

"He said he'll be on the road in front of your property at seven. He will let Teddy ride on his wagon with him as far as Falls Creek. The trader is staying at the inn for a few days to help Isaac prep the soil for winter wheat, so Revel will take Teddy the rest of the way home to Riverside."

John wedged a slip of paper into his Bible to mark his place. The binding clicked as he carefully closed his treasured book. "I am pleased the trader will travel with you back to Falls Creek. By our traditions you and Revel must have a chaperone when you travel, especially now that you are courting."

Bailey forgot about watching the stairs and curled her feet onto the sofa cushion, the gentle crackle of the fire luring her to stay right here forever. "Courting… chaperones… traditions. This will be complicated. Worth it, but complicated."

"Not to worry. The ladies at the inn will be good advisors for you." He steepled his fingers. "They will not let you do anything that might sully your reputation, such as traveling with Revel unchaperoned."

Bailey thought of the greenhouse at Falls Creek and the winter plants she needed to sow. "I'll have so much to do when I get home; I don't think I'll have time to go on the road with Revel very much. But I'll see him often since he plans to keep his routes short until the haze is gone." She looked toward the curtained window. Though night had fallen hours ago, she could still imagine the blurry cloud that ringed the horizon. "Not that we expect it to darken the Land. It's been a month since the volcanic eruptions occurred, and there is still no ash cloud directly above us."

"So you do not believe the Land is in danger of the long freeze Mr. Mercer warned us about?"

"No, I don't. Connor agrees with me that the clear skies above are proof the haze will not affect the Land's atmosphere. But since the haze is still on the horizon, I advised all the overseers to make sure my crop recommendations are carried out. Better safe than sorry, right?"

"In this circumstance, yes." John pressed his lips together in a thoughtful line. "And I too believe we are safe here."

She found a fingernail edge that was long enough to bite, but she didn't feel the urge. "So does Lydia. She thinks our protection from the ash has to do with the gray leaf molecules in the air and the atmospheric anomaly around the Land."

He gently laid his Bible on a side table beside a glowing lantern. "Remember the passage from the eighth chapter of Romans? Verse twenty-eight?"

This time she didn't need to close her eyes to envision the underlined sentence in her Bible. "*And we know that all things work together for good to them that love God, to them who are the called according to His purpose*."

John nodded approvingly. "We can trust God to work all circumstances for our good, even volcanic ash clouds and atmospheric anomalies."

He spoke of things he'd never had to consider before outsiders were swept into this hidden land, and he spoke with the clarity of understanding that befitted a lifelong scholar no matter the era. Lydia had inherited that quality from him.

Bailey wished she could stay longer to run more gray leaf experiments with Lydia. "I worked with great researchers in America, and Lydia's capabilities exceed them all. Sometimes, when I get her letters about her research, her observations of the gray leaf astound me."

John smiled at the praise of his daughter. "I am blessed to be surrounded by brilliant minds, including yours."

She pointed at herself. "I don't know about brilliant over here. I enjoy working with Lydia, and we have solid theories." She unfurled her legs and stretched them out along the sofa cushions. "It would have been nice if I could have stayed here the whole season, but I want to get home to prep the greenhouse and follow my own recommendations."

John scratched his trimmed gray beard. "You have done much good for the Land while you were here, Bailey."

She thought about her few weeks in Good Springs, and her chest grew heavy with her only regret. She lowered her volume just in case anyone was still awake in the house. "Not everything I did here was good. When I found Justin Mercer on the shore, I thought my life in the

Land was over. I honestly wanted to kill Koslov. To me, he represented all of Global and everything that destroyed life outside the Land, but that's no excuse for what was in my heart."

"The flesh is always at war with the spirit. But you armed yourself with God's Word. He honored that."

John's gracious words lifted the last weight from her heart. "Yes, I suppose He did."

He angled his head. "You came to Good Springs with questions, and you aren't staying as long as you had planned. Did you find your answers while you were here?"

She pictured the stack of scripture cards she had tied with a bit of ribbon and tucked into the side pocket of her backpack. She'd yet to memorize all the verses, but she would. Though the truth in those scriptures had given her much peace, the unsettled feelings she'd carried to Good Springs stemmed from something much more basic… more natural than spiritual.

She kept her voice quiet, but answered John with all confidence. "I was yearning for something I couldn't define. And I couldn't define it because I wasn't letting myself even consider it. I thought since I could protect myself and provide for myself, I didn't need a man. But loving someone deeply and being loved *and* being understood by that person… it's unbelievable. Revel didn't have the answer; he is the answer."

John folded his hands restfully, the way he did when he closed his Sunday sermons. "Two are truly better than one."

"Amen."

"I pray God's very best for the two of you."

"That means a lot to me." She stood and retracted her hands into her sweatshirt sleeves, ready to snuggle under the quilt in her borrowed bedroom for her last night at the Colburn house. "Good night, John. And thank you for everything."

EPILOGUE

The afternoon sun's fading rays darted through the strong limbs of an ancient gray leaf tree that guarded the cemetery near Falls Creek. Bailey petted her horse's mane as she rode over the stone bridge after the long journey across the Land. "Good girl, Gee. We made it home."

Revel, riding close enough beside her that their stirrups almost touched, gave her a side glance. "Home. It's nice to hear you say that."

The beautiful inn stood before them, both of their lonely pasts behind them. A warm layer of peace surrounded Bailey. "It feels like everything I wanted my whole life is finally mine to keep—home, family, friends… you."

Revel's chest lifted with a strong inhale. He blew it out between smiling lips. "I've waited a long time too."

As they rode onto the bare dirt in front of the inn, Revel waved the trader's wagon to go around them to the stable block where wagons parked. Young Teddy Vestal was sitting beside the trader, still talking at full speed. The young man truly had missed being around people. He wanted to go off on his adventures, but he was too social to stay alone for long. After the wagon passed them,

Bailey pointed at it and said to Revel, "He is a lot like you."

"Teddy? Yeah. I reckon he will be riding the trade routes as soon as his parents let him."

Bailey swung down from Gee and looped her rope through the hitching post by the inn's front steps, but Revel lingered in Blaze's saddle for a moment. He knocked his hat higher with a knuckle and gazed down at her, eyes full of hope. "Come with me."

She was in the middle of stretching her stiff leg muscles from three days of horseback riding. "Now?"

His feet hit the dirt with alacrity as he hopped down from Blaze. "Not now, but soon."

"To Riverside?" A strand of hair fell across her vision as she shook her head. "No, you need to get Teddy home to his parents and I have work to do here. Besides, John told me not to travel with you without a…" she could hardly believe she was saying the word, "chaperone. Since we're courting now or whatever you call this."

He chuckled faintly as he rounded his horse and met her by the porch steps. "That's what I'd call it… for now."

The closer he came, the closer she wanted him to be. "I'm not really into labels and traditions and all that." When his eyes darkened, she slid her hands up his shoulders. "I just know I want to be with you. In life—always. On the road—occasionally."

He lowered his smiling lips to hers. "That's fine with me." He kissed her once, then softly repeated himself, "For now."

The inn's heavy wooden door rattled open, and Eva blew onto the porch like a corner-office CEO on her way to a board meeting. "What's this, then? Are the two of you kissing on the porch like a couple of lovebirds?" The edge in her voice was betrayed by the grin on her face. "Has Sybil's prayer finally been answered?"

Bailey pulled away from Revel and wiped her lips, but he didn't move an inch. He only cocked his head at his sister and returned her playful quip. "Mind your own business, woman."

Eva propped her thin fists on her hips, but her smile only grew. "What goes on at this inn *is* my business, you filthy nomad."

Before Bailey could laugh, Sybil whirled through the doorway. "Bailey! Revel! You're back!" She flitted down the steps then stopped near Bailey and braced herself with a hand on the post. "Oh, dear."

Bailey steadied Sybil with both hands. "You okay, Syb?"

Sybil put a hand to her middle and gave a nervous chuckle. "I'm fine." She glanced at Eva and Revel, then looked Bailey in the eye with a happy but sickly smile. "Or at least I will be fine in about seven more months."

Bailey squeezed her arms gently, unsure if a hug would make her friend's nausea worse. "Congratulations! I'll bet Isaac is thrilled."

"He's already built the baby's cradle."

While Bailey walked Sybil up the porch steps, the trader and Teddy ambled over from the stable block where they'd parked the wagon. Revel made the introductions and tousled Teddy's hair as he told his sisters who the young man was.

Sybil excused herself, and Eva and the trader bartered terms for his stay at the inn. While Eva showed him to her office to get his room key, Revel stopped Teddy at the door. "Let's make a deal too."

"What kind of deal?"

"How about if you promise to mind your parents and don't leave home without telling them, I'll talk to them about taking you on my courier route with me occasionally. That way you can have your adventures and your parents won't have to fret."

Teddy squared his shoulders the way fourteen-year-old boys did when they wanted to be seen as men. "Sounds like a fair deal to me."

Revel shook his hand. "Maybe you'll take a liking to the courier business. It's a great way to see the countryside, but it's important to have someone to come home to." He finished his sentence looking at Bailey instead of the young man.

Teddy rolled his eyes. "I don't think he's talking to me anyone."

While the boy went inside the inn, Revel stayed on the porch. "He catches on quick."

"I'm impressed. You're great with him."

Revel pointed at himself and crinkled a questioning brow, but smiled. "Me?"

"Yes, you. I think you'll be a good influence in his life over the years."

"Wow… *years*. I never think of anything in terms of years."

"Sometimes it takes years to arrive at a single moment." She looked up at the sign over the inn's door, a snippet from one of her favorite Bible verses. *Find rest for your souls.*

Revel looked up at the sign too. His low voice had never sounded so sure. "That never made sense to me until now."

"The sign?"

He shook his head, slowly, thoughtfully. "How people always said they felt at peace here. I never felt that," he looked down at her, "until now. It's you, Bailey. It's always been you and will always be you. And when you're ready, we will walk over there to the chapel and ask Philip to marry us. Then I'll build you a little house on our land down the road if you want. You can come with me on my route whenever you feel like it or stay here and spend your days in the greenhouse, dusted with fertilizer and happiness." He turned the doorknob with one hand and offered the other to her. "As long as I know you're here, Falls Creek will always be my home too."

No sweeter words had ever seeped into her heart, his love softening her scars, his friendship delighting her soul.

She gave the hazy horizon one last glance, then took Revel's waiting hand. "No matter what happens out there, we are safe here and we are home."

Thank you for reading my book. I'm so glad you went on this journey with me. More Uncharted stories await you! Are you ready for the adventure?

I know it's important for you to enjoy these wholesome, inspirational stories in your favorite format, so I've made sure all of my books are available in ebook, paperback, and large print versions.

Below is a quick description of each story so that you can determine which books to order next…

The Uncharted Series
A hidden land settled by peaceful people ~ The first outsider in 160 years

The Land Uncharted (#1)
Lydia's secluded society is at risk when an injured fighter pilot's parachute carries him to her hidden land.

Uncharted Redemption (#2)
When vivacious Mandy is forced to depend on strong, silent Levi, she must learn to accept tender love from the one man who truly knows her.

Uncharted Inheritance (#3)
Bethany and Everett belong together, but when a mysterious man arrives in the Land, everything changes.

Christmas with the Colburns (#4)
When Lydia faces a gloomy holiday in the Colburn house, an unexpected gift brightens her favorite season.

Uncharted Hope (#5)
While Sophia and Nicholas wrestle with love and faith, a stunning discovery outside the Land changes everything.

Uncharted Journey (#6)
When horse trainer Solo moves to Falls Creek, widow Eva gets a second chance at love. Meanwhile, Bailey's quest to reach the Land costs her everything.

Uncharted Destiny (#7)
The Uncharted story continues when Bailey and Revel face an impossible rescue mission in the Land's treacherous mountains.

Uncharted Promises (#8)
When Sybil and Isaac get snowed in, it takes more than warm meals and cozy fireplaces to help them find love at the Inn at Falls Creek.

Uncharted Freedom (#9)
When Naomi takes the housekeeping job at The Inn at Falls Creek to hide from one past, another finds her.

Uncharted Courage (#10)
With the survival of the Land at stake and their hearts on the line, Bailey and Revel must find the courage to love.

Uncharted Christmas (#11)
While Lydia juggles her medical practice and her family obligations this Christmas, she is torn between the home life she craves and the career that defines her.

Uncharted Grace (#12)
Caroline and Jedidiah must overcome their shattered pasts and buried secrets to find love in the village of Good Springs.

The Uncharted Beginnings Series
Embark on an unforgettable 1860s journey with the Founders as they discover the Land.

Aboard Providence (#1)
When Marian and Jonah's ship gets marooned on a mysterious uncharted island, they must build a settlement to survive. Love and adventure await!

Above Rubies (#2)
When schoolteacher Olivia needs the settlement elders' approval, she must hide her dyslexia from everyone, even charming carpenter Gabe.

All Things Beautiful (#3)
Henry is the last person Hannah wants reading her story… and the first person to awaken her heart.

Find out more on my website keelybrookekeith.com or feel free to email me at keely@keelykeith.com where I answer every message personally.

See you in the Land!
Keely

ABOUT THE AUTHOR

Keely Brooke Keith writes inspirational frontier-style fiction with a slight Sci-Fi twist, including *The Land Uncharted* (Shelf Unbound Notable Romance 2015) and *Aboard Providence* (2017 INSPY Awards Longlist).

Born in St. Joseph, Missouri, Keely was a tree-climbing, baseball-loving 80s kid. She grew up in a family who moved often, which fueled her dreams of faraway lands. When she isn't writing, Keely enjoys teaching home school lessons and playing bass guitar. Keely, her husband, and their daughter live on a hilltop south of Nashville, Tennessee.

For more information or to connect with Keely, visit her website www.keelybrookekeith.com.

Made in the USA
Middletown, DE
21 October 2023

41178068R00144